Under the Hollies

What tale did Iseult to the children say,
Under the hollies, that bright winter's day?
MATTHEW ARNOLD : *Tristram and Iseult*

UNDER
THE HOLLIES

Laurence Meynell

Illustrated by
IAN RIBBONS

Geoffrey Cumberlege
OXFORD UNIVERSITY PRESS
1954

Oxford University Press, Amen House, London, E.C.4
GLASGOW NEW YORK TORONTO MELBOURNE WELLINGTON
BOMBAY CALCUTTA MADRAS KARACHI CAPE TOWN IBADAN
Geoffrey Cumberlege, Publisher to the University

First published 1954

PRINTED IN GREAT BRITAIN BY
MORRISON AND GIBB LIMITED, LONDON AND EDINBURGH

Contents

For my godson
NIGEL MUERS-RABY
in the hope that one day
he will enjoy reading it

PART ONE

ROAD-MAKERS

(*Roman* : A.D. *125*)

It's funny how things happen. Young Tom Reid's parents were going to Australia on a visit for four months. After a good deal of discussion they had decided to take Tom with them and everything was more or less fixed up. Two weeks after the final fixing up, and shortly before the trip itself was due to start, the three of them—Mr and Mrs Reid and Tom—went to the circus.

When Mr Reid went to book seats the only ones left were three in the very front row, right next to the raised edge of the ring.

Mrs Reid said : ' Oh dear, that's frightfully close ' ; Tom said : ' Jolly good, the nearer the better ' ; and Mr Reid said : ' Well, they're the only ones there are, so it's them or nothing.'

So that evening they all three went to the circus and sat in the front row, up against the ring.

The third turn of the evening was a young Arab horse running free and jumping. It was a clever, tricky little pony and it jumped as neatly as a cat. First of all the attendants held up a series of light wooden hoops about two feet off the ground, through which it jumped in turn ; then they held the same wooden hoops horizontally, with one end of each resting on the raised edge of the ring, and the pony was supposed to do a series of in-and-out jumps : *up, down* ; *up, down* ; *up, down* ; jumps which had to be done very quickly and which were not easy to manage.

Tom wasn't particularly fond of horses anyway, and although he was interested enough in what was happening he was really waiting for the elephants and the lions to come on. Which meant that he wasn't leaning forward in his seat as he might have been ; and, as things turned out, that was lucky for him, because, having cleared three of the in-and-out jumps successfully, the quick-moving pony fouled the last one and sent the light wooden hoop spinning out of the attendant's hand.

It shot across the short distance of about four feet, which was all that separated the ring from the front row of seats, and caught Tom half on his arm and half across his chest.

There was quite a commotion, of course ; and the final result was that Tom was laid up with a terrific bruise on the muscle part of his left arm, which didn't really matter very much ; and two broken ribs, which did. At any rate it mattered sufficiently to prevent his going to Australia with his parents, and since they couldn't possibly put off their trip, which was for business reasons, and which was all fixed up anyway, something had to be done about Tom.

Young Tom, who was a quiet, undemonstrative sort of boy, took it all very philosophically.

'Don't you *mind* not going to Australia ? ' people asked him almost crossly.

'Well, not frightfully,' he confessed. 'It seemed a long way off, anyway. I daresay something else will turn up.'

What turned up was that Mrs Reid arranged with her married sister, Mrs Mason, to take Tom as a guest in her

4

house in Dallicombe for the necessary four months, so that the day before his father and mother flew from London Airport for Australia they put Tom on the West of England express at Paddington and said good-bye to him there.

Tom naturally had a good look at the locomotive before taking his seat, and was delighted to find that it was one of the Castle class (Dunster Castle 4093, actually ; coupled 4—6—0). He walked the length of the train, counted the coaches, and estimated that the weight behind the tender would be about four hundred and fifty tons.

These things he communicated to his mother, who, after the curious fashion of grown-ups, did not seem to consider them at all important.

' Now, *do* look after yourself, darling,' she said, ' and be nice to everybody. And change your clothes. And write to me occasionally. And don't go off into those dreamy fits of yours too often. You know what you are——'

Tom laughed. He was always getting into trouble with people for being ' dreamy ' ; but he couldn't help it ; and in fact he rather enjoyed it. But because his mother was going away for four months he thought he had better reassure her.

' I'll be most terribly good,' he promised.

The guard blew a long, warning whistle and suddenly Australia seemed very far off and four months a very long time.

' Good-bye, Mummy, good-bye.'

' Good-bye, darling.'

' Good-bye, Tom.'

' Good-bye, Dad.'

In the cabin of *Dunster Castle* the driver gave his regulator a slight push, steam eased through the superheater into the valve-heads, and almost imperceptibly the long train of fourteen coaches began to move.

Tom looked out of the window, partly because looking

5

out of the window was an exciting thing to do, and partly because he suddenly felt the need of seeing his parents for as long as possible.

Dad was grinning; and Mum, oh foolish Mum, was trying to wave and trying not to cry, and not being very successful at either. As a matter of fact, when Tom sat back in his seat, he felt just a little bit weepy himself for the first five minutes.

.   .   .   .   .

Reading, Newbury, Westbury, with a glimpse of a huge white horse cut out on a hillside, a fascinating and exciting thing, Frome, and then—

'Taunton,' the West Country porters were crying, only they made it sound more like 'Tarnton'.

Tom hadn't seen his Aunt Ella (Mrs Mason) or his cousins for more than three years and he had only the vaguest memory of what any of them looked like, so that he hardly knew whom to look out for.

He had been assured, however, that they would be there to meet him, so, having made sure that his trunk was put out of the guard's van, he sat down on it and waited philosophically until the crowd cleared away a bit.

When the crowd *had* cleared away and still nobody turned up to greet him he began to wonder what was wrong. *Taunton.* He was quite, quite certain that Taunton was the place where he had to get out; even in his dreamiest mood he surely couldn't be mistaken about that.

Besides, it said so on his ticket. So that was all right.

Perhaps they were outside the station, waiting for him there.

He wandered about a little (not altogether happy about leaving his trunk behind) but could see nobody who looked likely to be the Mason family.

'If anything happens, and you get lost, you have Aunt

6

Ella's telephone number, haven't you?' his mother had asked, not once, but half a dozen times.

'Yes, I have, Mums. Dallicombe 7.'

'And you do know how to use a telephone, one in a kiosk thing, I mean, don't you?'

'Don't be silly, Mums. I know much better than you do.'

Tom, recalling these conversations, was debating whether he had better try ringing up Dallicombe 7 when they arrived. Mrs Mason and her three children.

As soon as he saw Aunt Ella he remembered her. Bigger than Mums; with a fatter, whiter face; her hair rather vividly light in colour; perpetually out of breath but laughing a lot now and very welcoming and rather 'all over' him in a pleasant sort of way.

'Tom, I'm most frightfully sorry we are late. It was the wretched children who would go and look at a pony on the way here. Not that the animal is ever going to be the slightest use to us; but they would look at it. I do hope you haven't been waiting long.'

'Only a few minutes, thank you, Aunt Ella,' Tom said politely.

'Now come and make friends. It must be ages and ages since you children saw one another. Eleanor and Jennifer and Jump, this is your cousin Tom, and I want you all to make him welcome and to be particularly nice to him.'

Eleanor, aged fifteen, a dark, tall, thin girl; Jennifer, aged thirteen, just as dark but short and podgy; and Jump, a tough little chap aged eight, all viewed their cousin with intense curiosity, but without much sign of enthusiasm.

At length Eleanor said : 'Are you fond of horses?'

'Not frightfully, no,' Tom answered.

'Then what do you do all day?' Jennifer inquired.

Luckily this was a conversation which Mrs Mason missed, as she was busy getting a porter to see to Tom's trunk.

7

'Here we are,' she said, bustling back. 'Have you children been getting to know one another ? Good. Now, let's all get into the car and go home for tea.'

Dallicombe was an old-fashioned, sleepy, stone-built town which consisted, or so you thought at first glance, of the Square, an open space in front of the Town Hall, and the wide High Street. But when Tom looked a bit more closely, he realized that there were a lot of twisty, dark little openings off the High Street that looked as though they would lead to all sorts of interesting back parts.

Doctor Mason, like his father before him, lived in a big square house just outside the town itself. It had a name, Long Acre, but everybody in Dallicombe always called it ' the doctor's house ' and nothing else. There was a lawn and a wide herbaceous border in front, and at the back a long garden sloping gently down to a field and a small wood.

Tom liked it from the first moment he saw it. It felt friendly. And as the Austin turned in at the drive gate and he saw the house and the line of elms beyond, he experienced for a moment an odd sort of feeling.

' Have I been here before ? ' he asked, almost involuntarily.

' No. Never,' Mrs Mason laughed in her matter-of-fact way. ' We've been to see you a couple of times, but somehow you've never been down here. So it's high time you did come.'

This was not a sentiment with which any of the three Mason children agreed.

Normally they were a nice enough trio ; but as far as they were concerned, this visit of their practically unknown cousin Tom from the other side of England was an unfortunate affair. If cousin Tom had not been coming no less a person than Miss Dill would have visited them. And Miss Dill would have brought with her Hop-a-long and Velvet, her two celebrated gymkhana ponies.

'If Tom comes we can't possibly have Miss Dill,' had been Mrs Mason's dictum ; 'for one thing there isn't room, and for another, I simply cannot manage the work.'

'But must cousin Tom come ?'

'Of course he must. He's only just getting over two broken ribs, in fact he hasn't got over them yet. And his father and mother are going to Australia. What do you expect the poor boy to do ? I can't imagine what you children are thinking of.'

What they were thinking of, of course, was Hop-a-long and Velvet. But that was no good now and they had to put up with Tom Reid instead.

Tom knew nothing about Velvet, Hop-a-long, and Miss Dill ; but he did know, because he was a boy who felt atmospheres easily, that there was something wrong somewhere and that the children weren't tremendously pleased to see him.

So the first tea-time in Long Acre was rather a sticky affair ; but things cheered up a good deal when Doctor Mason came back from his afternoon rounds and immediately wanted to see Tom in the study.

Tom liked his uncle at once ; and he liked the study, too. It was a small, comfortable room with a large, deeply bowed window looking out on to the orchard, and hardly a square foot of wall visible because of the bookshelves that ran all round.

Doctor Charles Mason was a man of forty ; he was short and broad-shouldered, with the strong, capable hands of a surgeon ; he was the best cricket player Dallicombe had known for twenty years and a very good golfer ; and he had a smile that every man, woman, and child in the district was glad to see.

'Ah, Tom,' he cried, holding out his hand in welcome, 'I'm glad to see you here. So you arrived all right, eh ?'

'Yes, thank you, sir.'

And do you like the place, the house?'

'I think I do.'

'You haven't had much chance of seeing it yet, of course; and maybe you don't notice houses much anyway. Do you?'

Tom laughed a bit. 'I hardly know,' he said.

'Come on,' said his uncle, 'and I'll show you round.' 'Most of it is Georgian,' the Doctor said, 'and you can't beat Georgian for sensible, solid comfort. But of course there was something here in Georgian days already, and the back parts are mostly Tudor.'

And when they walked round to the yard and looked at the outside of the kitchen premises and some of the out-buildings, Tom spotted the solid oak timber work set between the narrow, handmade bricks, which had been doing duty there these four hundred years and more.

'Not that Tudor was the start of it,' the Doctor went on. 'Why should it be? England was grown-up by Henry VIII's day; she had seen a lot and forgotten a lot long before then. The cellars under the house—I'll take you down some day—are as old as billy-o. I should think that one way and another, people have been living here or hereabouts for just as long as they've been living anywhere in old England. I like that, you know: the feeling of layer after layer of history behind you. It makes you feel that you're standing on something, that you belong.'

Tom nodded: that was a feeling he could appreciate; and they moved off together down the garden.

'Heaven knows where those children of mine are,' the Doctor said. 'In the front paddock, I suppose, with the horse. Are you horse-mad, Tom?'

'No. Not really.'

'Thank heavens for that. It's a mercy to have somebody sane. Of course the garden isn't what it used to be. Albert Wilde, that's my gardener, does his best. He's a jolly good gardener—but then he's also eighty-two. And there are quite a lot of things you can't do when you're eighty-two, however willing you are. You try it.'

Tom laughed. He couldn't possibly imagine what being eighty-two could feel like.

By now they had walked past the small orchard with its load of apples ('You can keep the lot if you give me one tree of Laxton's Epicure,' Doctor Mason said. 'Maybe it won't keep, but it's the very best eating apple in the Good Lord's universe'), past the vegetable garden where an abundance of growing stuff bore testimony to Albert Wilde's activities despite his eighty-two years, and had reached the fence at the bottom.

'See the pond in the corner?' the Doctor asked. 'In the spring we always get a nest of moorhens on it. Whether some of the young ones come back each time to nest again on the pond where they were hatched out, I don't know. I'll have to find out some day. But we always have moorhens there and I like moorhens. Friendly, well-behaved things.'

Tom nodded. Then he exclaimed : 'What an odd old tree !'

The Doctor glanced up affectionately at the tree under which they were standing. Extreme age, to say nothing of various accidents and decay, had caused its great trunk to split into two boles, each as big as an ordinary good-sized tree, so that it was possible for any one to take shelter in the middle of it, or even to pass right through it.

'It's odd right enough,' Doctor Mason was saying. 'It must have been struck by lightning a couple of times, and there's a legend it was set on fire once. And *old* is right enough, too ; for that tree is certainly eight hundred years old and may well be a thousand.'

'Golly !'

'Yes. Funny to think that it was probably a lusty young

11

sapling when William of Normandy came ; and that it has seen all the changes that have happened to old England since.'

' But it's still alive ! ' Tom said.

The Doctor laughed. ' So's a man of a hundred still alive,' he answered, ' but he's on his last legs. Boller's Oak they call it locally, though nobody seems to know why. You see that flat part in the field ? '

Stretching away from the fence at the end of the garden, the fence in which the great oak stood, was a grazing meadow. It sloped down gently for a matter of a hundred yards and then, running right across it, there was a level width before it began to slope up again slightly to the hedge beyond.

' Why, it looks almost like a road,' Tom said.

' It *is* a road. At least it was. Heaven knows how long ago. And the Lord knows who built it. Might have been the Romans, might have been before them. I suppose it must have joined the main Exeter road somewhere in the valley, but nobody really knows. It's just one of the forgotten things.'

Tom lifted his eyes, and far away to the right he could see the moor stretching high up into the sky, and the late afternoon clouds making swift-moving shadows over its purple slopes. Tiny little white blobs, for all the world like white pinheads stuck in a purple pincushion, showed where Farmer Gleed's horned Exmoor sheep were grazing ; and a much tinier spot in the sky, too small for Tom to notice it, marked where a kestrel hovered expectantly, riding the air currents with consummate ease and grace.

' I'm going to like it here,' Tom said with a sudden conviction.

Doctor Mason nodded. ' Good man. That's the spirit. I hope you are.'

' When I first saw the house,' Tom began, ' I—I—'

The Doctor was watching him curiously. ' Go on, Tom,' he said, ' you what ? '

'Nothing really. Only I sort of felt I had been here before, somehow. Silly, of course, because I haven't.'

Doctor Mason didn't seem to think it an odd sort of remark to make at all.

'I'm not so sure it is silly,' he answered seriously. 'Have you ever thought about time, Tom? I mean, thought what it is exactly. Time's queer stuff, you know. Take the stars as an example. There are some of them so far off that it takes the light from them a thousand years to reach us; you probably knew that, didn't you?'

Tom nodded.

'But have you ever thought what it means? It means that tonight you and I are looking at something which was happening a thousand years ago. If the particular star blows up or explodes tonight we don't know anything about it here for another thousand years. And in the same way, what you and I are doing and saying now may not happen for somebody else for a hundred years or so.'

Tom stared at him, lost in thought.

'It is rum, isn't it?' he said at length.

'And this "I've-been-here-before" business,' the Doctor went on; 'I often think it may be true. We may all have lived before, different sort of lives in different sorts of ways. How do you know what you were before you were Tom Reid?'

'I was—I was nothing,' Tom said, a bit surprised, even a bit frightened.

'And, pray, just what is nothing?' Doctor Mason inquired. 'Can you define nothing? How can you be nothing? And if you were nothing, how did you suddenly become something?'

Tom stared at him again and then, giving it up, shook his head.

'I haven't a clue,' he confessed.

Doctor Mason threw his head back and roared with laughter.

'What a sensible answer,' he said. 'Neither has anybody else a clue, young Tom. Not the wisest philosopher in old

England. And the wiser he is, the more he would tell you that he hasn't, as you so succinctly put it, a clue. All he does know is that the rummiest things are liable to happen at times, and he certainly can't explain them.'

He stopped and chuckled and then started again. ' Ah, well, that's me off on my hobby-horse again. And I can hear six o'clock striking, which means surgery. I've got to get back to the house, Tom. You do what you like, of course ; either go and find the children in the front field, or knock about here on your own and explore. But you had better be in by half-past six, I guess ; or your aunt will probably be raising a row.'

'I'll be back long before then,' Tom promised. ' Is surgery exciting ? '

Doctor Mason made a face. 'Not very. Headaches, tummy-aches, backaches, leg-aches—the whole human body creaking away. You get rather tired of it at times. I'd sooner stay out here with you and watch the moorhens.'

As soon as his uncle had left him, Tom began to explore. He went to the pond first of all, and there was the now disused moorhens' nest sticking up boldly and baldly on a small clump of reeds right in the middle of it. He didn't see the dapper little moorhens themselves, but presently he was aware of a bright eye watching him expectantly from the hedge.

' Hallo, robin,' he said.

But the robin didn't think much of him. In the robin's opinion anyone who came into that particular sector of the garden should have a spade and a fork and should be engaged in turning over the earth, thus bringing worms, small insects, and all sorts of interesting and edible things to light.

Tom was not doing any of this useful work, and the robin was disappointed in him. It said so plainly.

Next Tom examined the bonfire and was delighted to discover that, when he broke off a length from one of last year's bean sticks, which were stacked in a bundle against the oak, and

14

used it as a poker, the fire, which had looked completely dead, came to life again and thin wisps of bluey-grey smoke began to creep out of it and curl lazily upwards in the evening air.

So then, of course, he had to get some dry leaves and some bits of stick and play about until he managed to get a little, quick, gobbling-up flame showing at one side of it.

And since friend Fire is one of the oldest and one of the best and one of the most terrible playthings in the world, the minutes slipped by quickly enough; the robin gave up waiting for anything worthwhile to happen and went away in disgust; and the first darkness of evening began to steal out on quiet grey feet from the woods and from the fields and from the very air itself.

The little spurt of flame that Tom had managed to induce died away, discouraged by too much wet grass; and he lost interest in the fire. He straightened up, and was suddenly aware of coolness in the air.

'One more look at the old oak,' he thought, 'and then I'll go in.'

This time he climbed—it was really not much more than a step—right into the middle of the old tree.

'What a marvellous little place you could make for yourself in here,' he thought.

Then he pushed through farther and, moving a small, low-down branch to one side, looked out on the meadow beyond.

Moving the branch had been almost like drawing a green curtain to one side. At one moment you couldn't see the field, and the next there it was laid out before you, framed in the bole of the great oak, as though it were a picture, or a stage when the curtain goes up and the play begins. . . .

And instantly Tom was aware of something happening. Evening mist was beginning to come up from the stream beyond and to float over the meadow, and in the mist, figures, insubstantial and wraith-like themselves, were moving.

15

There were men and horses, and a gleam for an instant as though sunlight from far away and long ago was glinting on armour, and a sudden shout that sounded as though it came from the morning of Time.

All this didn't seem odd to Tom in the slightest. Somehow it seemed quite natural. It certainly didn't frighten him. He was fascinated by it, and he stood there gripping the bole of the great oak and staring out at the field, which seemed full of people, and of shouting and of movement. . . .

He might have stood like that for one minute or for ten. Time was funny stuff, he remembered Doctor Mason saying . . . then from half-way up the garden path behind he heard a voice, very practical, very modern and up-to-date :

' Tom, Tom, where are you ? Time to come in.'

It was Aunt Ella ; and at her voice Tom turned his head quickly and called : ' Coming, Aunt Ella.'

When he looked once more at the field for a final glance there was nothing there ; only the vague darkness of the trees in the spinney beyond and the white evening mist, now thickening, over the grass.

' Coming, Aunt Ella,' Tom called again ; and she was satisfied. But what he really meant, of course, was that he was coming back *there*, to the oak through which you could climb, from which you could look out on the enchanted field ; the field in which Time Stood Still.

.   .   .   .   .

Two days after Tom came to Dallicombe there was a meet of the mid-Somerset at Vail's Cross.

All three Mason children were going as a matter of course. They couldn't imagine a meet of the foxhounds taking place within ten miles to which they wouldn't go.

Eleanor rode Timber, a chestnut that was really too big for her, and a bit of a handful, but beloved by her over all other horses, real or imagined, and certainly better-behaved with her than he would have been with anybody else.

Jennifer had Cinders—a narrow-backed, quick-stepping, well-bred little thing that could go like the wind ; and Jump was out on Polly, as broad as a kitchen-table and as good-natured and well-behaved as a circus horse.

Mrs Mason was going to be away all day at a meeting of the Women's Institute in Taunton.

'Heaven knows what poor Tom will do,' she said, rather upset about leaving him alone. 'Do you think he could go hunting, Harry, if we found him something to ride ?'

'He cannot go hunting,' Doctor Mason said firmly, 'not if you got Foxhunter himself for the boy to ride. He's getting over two broken ribs and he's to take things easily. From what I've seen of him, he'll be quite happy messing about in the garden all day.'

And when Mrs Mason tackled Tom himself on the subject, he said the very same thing to her.

'I shall be perfectly all right knocking about in the garden. Please don't worry about me in the slightest, Aunt Ella.'

'You're sure ?' Mrs Mason asked, still a bit doubtful.

'Perfectly sure.'

Breakfast was a noisy affair, with all three Mason children in a ferment of excitement — particularly Eleanor, whose jodhpurs had suddenly disclosed a hitherto undiscovered hole which must ('simply must, it's an Inescapable Must, Mummy') be sewn up at once.

But things got sorted out in time and Mrs Mason bundled herself into her own small car and set off, not more than twenty minutes late, for Taunton and her day with the W.I.

Half an hour later the other children rode out of the drive gate : Timber showing the whites of his excited eyes more than a little, Cinders making music with her small, dainty feet, Polly steady and entirely composed.

Tom stood in the drive to watch them go.

'Sorry you aren't coming,' Eleanor said, as Cinders sidled past.

'That's all right.'

'Don't have too mouldy a time all by yourself,' Jump said from on top of broad-backed Polly.

'No fear, I won't. I shall be all right.'

Half an hour after the children had gone, Doctor Mason started out on his morning round in the Austin.

'Sorry to leave you, Tom,' he called out breezily. 'Poke about wherever you want to. I may be a bit late for lunch, but Liza will see you're all right.'

'That's fine,' Tom answered. 'Thanks a lot.'

He watched the Austin sweep out of the entrance gate on to the road and then turned back to the house with the pleasant, exciting feeling of having the place to himself.

Of course he wasn't entirely by himself. There was Liza in the kitchen; but he had already learnt that it was better to keep out of those regions.

If you met Liza outside the kitchen she was a nice, homely, friendly body; but if you made the mistake of going into her territory she grumbled at you like a bomb about to explode at any moment.

So Tom mooched round to the back, where Albert Wilde was digging in the vegetable garden, forking-in a compost of rotted grass and leaves and chicken manure as he went. He and Tom had already made friends, and the old man was glad enough of an excuse to stop work for a moment and ease his back.

'Good morning, Mr Wilde,' Tom said politely.

'Mus' Tom.'

Tom looked with interest at the barrow-load of rotted material that the old man had just wheeled up from the compost heap.

'That looks jolly good stuff,' he said.

18

''Tis. No sense in starving the old girl. If you keep a-taking good out of 'er you must keep a-putting good into 'er. Only sense. The old makes the new, that's how 'tis, Mus' Tom.'

It suddenly struck Tom that Albert was in some ways remarkably like the great oak-tree at the bottom of the garden.

'How old is the oak, Mr Wilde ?' he asked.

Albert laughed. 'No telling, Mus' Tom. Not really to rights. Doctor did have a clever chap down 'ere once as belonged to some sociation or such like, and he had a look at 'er, and took his eye-glasses off and held them swinging in his hand and read a bit out of a book, and said as she was eight hunder and fifty-three years ancient.'

The old man gave a peculiar guffaw at the memory. 'I could a' laffed myself fit to bust,' he went on, ' this Lunnon sociation chap talking so solemn and the Doctor standing there a-taking it all in. Maybe the sociation chap was right, though. But Tinker Deane as works in the woods—well, Woodman Deane he should be called to rights, along with his father before him, and *his* father and *his*; the Deanes always have been woodmen hereabouts, I reckon, since a very tidy bit agoo —Tinker Deane, he came up to see me one day over a little matter of rabbits—no names, no pack-drill, as they say—and he a-stuck his ferretty little head into the middle of 'er, and sniffed a bit and touched the bole of 'er with his hand, and walked round 'er slowly like a man 'ud walk round a hoss at the hoss fair before buying, and *'e* said "if she's a day she's a thousand year old, and a bit over for good measure, I wouldn't wonder".'

'Golly !'

Albert plunged the five rounded and shining tines of his fork into the barrow-load of gently steaming compost.

'Eight hunder and fifty-three or a thousand, don't sinnify much what I can see of it one way or t'other. We shall all be safe in churchyard before a tenth o' that lot comes round again. 'Tis a mighty long lot of years anyway, and the old

19

tree has seen a bit in her time, standing up there and a-looking out over Street Meadow like she does.'

' Street Meadow ? '

' That's the name of the meadow at the bottom.'

' Why ever do they call it " Street Meadow " ? '

' Ah well, now,' Albert Wilde said, bending to his work again, ' there's every field in old England has its proper lawful name and calling, and if we was to know the why and wherefore of all of them I doubt we should learn a bit.'

Tom watched the old man turning the soil and forking-in the compost for some time, and eventually, after exploring the pond pretty thoroughly, he finished up by the oak.

The old tree stood there like a scarred veteran of time, still sturdy in spite of all the vicissitudes that had befallen it, and managing somehow to seem very friendly.

As Tom approached it, he was conscious at the back of his mind that Dallicombe church clock was chiming the hour. Eleven o'clock already, he supposed it must be ; and the actual strokes had just begun—he had counted three of them— as he began to climb into the middle of the tree.

The funny thing was that when he got into the tree he didn't seem to hear any more of the strokes of the church clock. *One, two, three.* . . . They had been coming clear and distinct to his ears on the morning air, and then he was aware of them no more.

Instead, the atmosphere all around him was suddenly vibrant with—with *what* ? He wasn't quite sure. Was it a noise exactly ? And if so, what noise ? Water running ? Wheels turning backward ? Neither of these ; or both of them mixed up, maybe ?

Whatever it was, the air quivered with it in a suddenly exciting way, and Tom's throat contracted a little in anticipation as he laid his hand on the green bough before him and moved it to one side so that he could see the field. . . .

20

It was bright and blustery. A blue sky, with great billowy white clouds fairly racing across it. You didn't have to look at the black ash-beds to be sure it was March. You knew it was March in your veins. A lovely, sunny March day with a cold wind blowing and the whole earth starting to turn again.

And the field full of men busy working.

The boy caught his breath. All his ten years he had longed to see this sight, yet by chance and accident he never had as yet. He lived in a remote place, and he was but a swineherd's brat ; and so far the boundaries of his world had been the hovel where he slept and the hamlet where he tended the pigs.

Now he was looking at the Legendary Thing. This was what he had longed to see, and he feasted his eyes on the sight.

He made a rough counting. It wasn't easy to be exact, for some were in the wood and some were down where the bullock carts were unloading. And in any case they weren't very many ; but they seemed a lot, of course, to a boy who frequently spent a whole long day in the open without setting eyes on another human being.

The legionaries were easy to count. Two finger-lots of

those. No more. More? The boy didn't want more; couldn't imagine more. Ten tall, sturdy men with the sun glinting bravely off their polished bronze helmets and off the cunning, overlapping bronze armour that protected, without hampering, their shoulders and chests. True, they had piled arms, that is, they had stacked their shields, their long iron-headed javelins, and their short, lethal swords in the wood nearby out of the sun, and to that extent were the less soldiers for the moment.

But the watching boy knew nothing of that. To his un-instructed eyes they made a brave enough showing as they were. He had never in his life seen anything like this before. He had heard about it and dreamed about it. Now he was looking at it. And it came up to all expectation. It exceeded all belief. *This was Rome.* The Romans. The people to whose world he already felt himself to belong, and to which he wanted to belong still further. The legendary people who were stronger than nature herself, who could build (he had heard the marvels talked about) not one house of stone only, but whole towns of such houses ; who marched, not on tracks and footpaths that had to twist and turn to miss a swamp or dodge a thicket, but on wide straight roads laid across the land like a pointing stick ; who, when they camped at night, camped four square and solid ; big men who laughed and went unafraid, and talked of wider skies and of incredible things beyond the sea which their long ships crossed so certainly and so regularly.

All this the boy knew by report ; and now he looked at them. The Romans. *Rome*—the word was like wine in his throat, a magic. He was a little bit afraid ; but to balance that, and to out-balance it, he was immensely curious.

After a moment's hesitation he began to walk across the scrub-covered ground towards them, not even bothering to notice whether he trod on the prickly furze or not, for his

22

bare brown feet, which had never known a covering, were so hard that nothing hurt them.

As he drew near, his quick eyes sorted out more details.

Besides the legionaries there were also the auxiliaries. Many more of them. Four or five double handfuls in the count. These were his own kind, of course. The kind he lived with, the kind he was.

Short and swarthy. They had a uniform, Rome's uniform, but there was no armour in it. Rope sandals for their feet and a stout leather jerkin for their bodies was what they wore. They were in the service of Rome, in the pay of Rome, attached to the legions. They might go anywhere ; to places the boy had dimly heard of in his own land—Eburacum, Londinium, Lindum Colonia—and those seemed exciting enough. Or they might go in the long ships over the seas to a wide world that he hardly believed in. What a marvellous and exciting life, the boy thought, to attach yourself to a legion of the big and shining men, to go up and down the wide world wherever their tramping feet took them, to follow the Eagles, to be one with Rome.

The boy could see now what all this activity and commotion was about. But although he could see it, he still found it difficult to realize.

They were making a road.

In the hamlet where he lived in the swineherd's hut the women would sometimes in winter spend a day or so picking stones off the common field ; these they put into sacks and carried back to the hamlet, where they would be tipped out on to the muddiest patches of the footway. Sometimes in the worst of the weather the men would throw fallen branches of trees into the wheel-tracks in the borestall so that the carts would not get completely stuck in the mud ; and that was the extent of road-making as the boy knew it. When the known and worn path got too muddy, instinct and tradition told

23

them that the thing to do was to make a diversion slightly higher up the slope of the hill, so as to get away, if possible, from the water.

Now here was Rome making a road on the flat of the ground, actually next to the small stream that ran there.

The boy squatted down and watched. And as he watched he learnt much. He would have been very stupid and dull if he had not learnt, for things weren't done by talk and council-work here. Rome evidently did things in a different way. Here things were shipshape and clear-cut. Orders were given and they were carried out.

It was easy enough to spot who was giving the orders. Not that he shouted or ranted, that clearly wasn't Rome's way ; but every now and again one of the legionaries would go up to a sturdy figure standing close to the edge of the stream, salute, and talk for a minute or so.

When the question he brought had been answered, or his difficulty solved, he would salute again and go back to his place of work.

The sturdy man by the side of the stream looked older than any of the others, and a good deal older than most of them. He was dressed differently, too. His bronze helmet was plumed and the armour over the top half of his body was of a different design and more imposing.

Gossip heard in the hamlet, talk listened to in the ale-house of men who had been away from their homes and who came back bragging and boasting of what they had seen told the boy what this man was : he was no less a person than a centurion.

To the boy he was the very personification of Rome, the might and majesty of it. But actually he was only a middle-aged man, hard as hickory after following the Eagles for forty years, whose hair was now beginning to show grey under the stained straps of leather that came down on either side from his helmet and buckled beneath his chin.

UTH—C

What he was doing the boy could not at first make out. It might be some sort of game, though that seemed unlikely ; or a religious exercise, and that seemed much more probable. The boy well understood the necessity of placating the gods if you were to have any sort of good luck in whatever you might be doing ; the Sun, the Moon, Thor, Woden, and Frigga ; all these were deities with special days of their own, who had to be taken notice of if you wanted your affairs to thrive.

It seemed very probable, therefore, that the Centurion was doing something religious, and the boy watched him with interest.

He was standing close to a curious-looking contrivance. A pole of wood, maybe five feet high, was stuck in the ground and from the top of this four short, flat pieces stuck out, one pointing to each corner of the world. From the extremity of each of these flat pieces a cord was hanging down, kept taut by means of a blob of some kind—a stone or weight tied to the end of it.

It was this odd-looking thing which seemed to occupy all the Centurion's attention.

He continually lowered himself before it and gazed at it earnestly in a half-stooping position (some form of prayer, the boy guessed) and after he had done this for the space of half a dozen breaths he would throw up one of his arms, sometimes the right one, sometimes the left, and occasionally open or shut his hands quickly. When he had done this, looking down the little valley, he would step round to the other side of his pray-thing and repeat the performance looking in the opposite direction.

The boy was mystified. It was certainly not like any of the Thor and Woden stuff he was used to in the hamlet. Then he suddenly noticed something, and he could have kicked himself for not tumbling to it before.

There were others in this game, or god-worship, or whatever it might be.

As far as a medium bow-shot away a man stood, one of the auxiliaries, holding an upright piece of wood taller than himself and marked with a bit of furze tied to the top of it so that you could spot it easily. Not only was there this man, but there was another one beyond him, half a bow-shot farther on.

They were watching the Centurion and moving in accordance with his movements. If he held up his right arm they moved their upright sticks to that side ; or to the other side if he held up his left arm. When he kept one hand up and opened and shut the fingers of it, they still moved their sticks but only a very little.

When he had got them exactly where he wanted them he held both hands high up with his palms open and fingers stretched out ; and when this happened the man holding the upright marking-stick stuck the pointed end of it in the earth and stood slightly away from it.

Then the boy laughed at himself for thinking nonsense about god-worship. He could see now that all that was happening was that the Centurion was getting the four men with the tall marking-sticks (two in front of him and two behind) in an exactly straight line. The road was being set out. The two men behind stood on the centre of the part that was already laid and the two in front marked where the next portion would be.

' Ai, ai, ai,' the boy whistled softly to himself, delighted at his own perspicacity, and lost in amazement at all the new things he was seeing that bright March morning. ' So this is the trick of it.'

He turned his head and looked up the valley along the length of the road already made. In his heart he apologized to the tipplers and the boasters in the ale-house for ever imagining that they were exaggerating.

27

It was impossible to exaggerate what he saw. He tried to judge distances and widths with his eyes : two, three ox-carts certainly could go side by side on it, and then there would be space over. *Three ox-carts wide !* That he certainly would not have believed had somebody come telling of it. And as for length—he put up a strong brown hand to shield his eyes, for the valley ran away to the south-east and the sun was climbing. Wide and straight and flat—but not quite flat, he noticed, for it had a slight hump on its back, the road stretched away into the shimmering distance until his eyes were uncertain about it because of the dark woods that crowded down on either side.

Certainly it went as far as a horse could gallop without tiring and, as he realized in a flash of inspiration, it must go as far on beyond and as far again and again until it reached—where ? Rome itself maybe. All roads lead to Rome. He had heard the saying often enough, and now it leaped alive for him.

He got up and moved nearer to see how this Thing was being made. He went a little warily at first ; and then, since nobody seemed to be taking any notice of him, more boldly.

Where the direction of the road had already been laid out, the tall poles with their bits of furze atop stood marking the centre line.

At the right distance on either side of this centre line a trench had been dug showing the outside limits of the road, and going down as deep as its foundations were to be. All the soil between these two trenches was being moved. This in itself was an enormous job, and perhaps thirty of the auxiliaries were working on it.

The boy looked with envy at their tools. He was used to good tools in the hamlet, for there was a smith there very cunning in iron-work and a carpenter clever with wood ; but the things he knew and counted as good had not the solidity and massiveness of the picks and shovels these men were using.

There were eight auxiliaries working in each ditch on either side, with a legionary in charge of each gang. Not only in charge but working with them. Except for differences in dress there seemed little distinction between legionary and auxiliary.

'They all follow the Eagles,' the boy thought. 'They all serve Rome.'

The men dug, not swiftly, but with that persevering steadiness which in the course of a long day gets through so much. They were working in clay, and noticing this, the boy's face wrinkled in sympathetic amusement. He knew the clay. The hamlet stood on clay ; he had dug in it himself.

Every now and again a man would stop to take breath or ease his back for a moment and have a word with his mate ; or maybe the legionary in charge would walk along the line to see how things were going.

In between, in the space where the road itself would eventually come, where many tons of soil and stones had to be removed, there was also a deal of pick and shovel work, but horses were being used as well. This was full of interest for the boy. He was fond of horses and was accustomed to seeing them used for several things in the hamlet. Not infrequently they were put to the plough, although the older men on the council still preferred the oxen, especially in the clay. A horse was always used for harrow-work after the plough ; and a pack-horse with a wicker basket slung on either side was the usual way of carrying loads.

But here there was something different.

Five auxiliaries with picks went first in a row ; they worked with quick, short strokes, not striking too deep but loosening the earth for a depth of two hands or so. When they had finished their work they stood to one side, resting on their picks.

29

Then came the scrapers. A scraper was a long board about a foot and a half high, resting on the ground and guided by a man at the back holding a wooden handle. The board was pulled by four horses and was set at an angle so that as the loose earth mounted up before it, it was half carried, half pushed to one side all the time. An auxiliary with a whip was in charge of each team of horses. He needed his whip, for it was hard work, and once a drag had started it was fatal to let the team stop in the middle.

By means of these scrapers all, or at any rate most, of the earth which the pick-men had loosened was gradually worked to the sides, where it stood in mounds some three feet high waiting to be shifted away.

Watching all this with fascinated and intelligent eyes, the boy thought that it was lucky for the Centurion that the weather was dry, for in the wet this horse-and-board business would never work. Then, especially in the clay, it would have to be all patient spade work, and the slower for it.

Some distance behind the horses and scrapers, where pick and shovel had cleared everything away and got down to the required depth, the real business of building the road itself was going slowly forward.

Here, the boy noticed, there were three legionaries and three auxiliaries working together, and the legionaries were doing most of the actual work. This was skilled mason's work ; craft. This was the essence of the road, and Rome was not taking any chances with it.

The boy, bold enough by this time to come right up close to the edge of things, looked on with large solemn eyes, his capacity for wonder by this time exhausted.

First, right down into the bottom, when the rammers had beaten the surface hard and true, went the foundation. This was made of large stones, slab-like in shape and some so big that they were lowered the necessary five feet by short ropes.

These stones were not just thrown in higgledy-piggledy, the way the hamlet women tipped their pigmy pebbles on the miry parts of the paths. The foundations of the road were dealt with one by one, the masons fitting them patiently by hand and considering each individual stone carefully to see where it would best fit and lie.

This was slow work, and the boy noticed particularly that the legionary in charge of it would not let the next step be taken until he was absolutely satisfied that *his* work, the foundation, was right.

When he had passed a length of foundation work as being finished, the middle part of the road was tipped in on top of it. This consisted of much smaller stones, with broken Roman bricks or smashed tiles among them ; these were carried in sacks to the edge of the construction work and then tipped out.

This stuff was not dealt with individually and slowly as the foundation stones had been. Such careful treatment was not necessary or even desirable here. This was the middle part of the road, the core of it, which was not going to be subject to actual contact with either weather or traffic, and which must not be bound too tightly. A certain amount of elasticity was necessary in it to give spring to the road as a whole.

There was a length where as much of this central core as was needed had been put in, and here the boy saw something which for a moment or two puzzled him greatly.

No fewer than four oxen were drawing it. They were harnessed abreast ; four oxen abreast was a thing he had not seen before, and he thought at first that they were pulling a very curious sort of cart. It had three wheels side by side, but they were wheels of the oddest kind, being very low and very broad. Across the top of the wheels was laid a massive length of tree trunk, a solid bole of oak.

But why should the oxen be dragging an oak-tree into the middle of the road ? And, much more mysterious still, why, having dragged it so far infinitely slowly and laboriously, should they be turned and made to drag it back again ?

Had Rome gone mad, he wondered, watching the mysterious evolutions in astonishment ; then once again he gave the little cry under his breath.

' Ai, ai, ai,' he called, wondering anew at his own stupidity. It was only necessary, he realized suddenly, to see what the top of the rubble filling looked like after the oxen and their heavy load had creaked laboriously over it to know the answer to it all.

The oak-tree was there for its weight, and the wheels were made broad like that to squash as many stones as possible ; and where the broad wheels and the heavy tree had been, the top of the rubble was pressed down comparatively flat and even. The boy had never seen that done before ; it was a new trick for the hamlet.

' Ai, ai, ai,' he said again. ' That too, eh ? '

He watched and saw the sharp-pointed goad-stick at work, and heard the shouts of the auxiliary in charge of the oxen.

' Hard on the beasts, though,' the boy thought, ' pulling over those stones.'

Hard work it was ; but, on the other hand, and the boy realized it, the oxen he was used to in the hamlet were not such as these, who were fat and sleek and obviously well-fed on the best of food ; and they were shod. He could see the iron on their feet.

' Rome looks after her beasts, then, as well as her men,' he thought ; and it was even truer than he knew. Cut into the hair on the flank of every ox working on the site was a mark and a number ; the mark of its legion and a number for the beast itself. A thousand miles away in Rome, actually on the top shelf in a long, dark office in the basement of the Army Records Department, in the Via Augusta, there was a book in which, among many thousands of others, the legion mark and the number of that particular ox was entered.

Every third month each of the sixty centurions in the legion told his superior officer, a military tribune, how many men he had serving under him ; how they were divided, into legionaries or auxiliaries ; which had married women of the Britons ; if any were sick and in what hospital ; if any had been punished and why. And besides the tale of men, the centurions must render also a list of vehicles, goods, and animals. Each of the six military tribunes of the legion in turn rendered his fuller account to the officer commanding the whole legion, no less than a full legate. And in due course the officer commanding sent the full return to Rome. It went by the Imperial Post, wet or fine, summer or winter, covering thirty-five miles every twenty-four hours, along the great Roman roads without let or hindrance, stoppage or delay, until it arrived in Rome.

And the legate who sent off that three-monthly report was often enough a little nervous about the sort of reception it would get in the Roman War Office.

He might be a very powerful person within his own legion ; he might be a little god there, but away back in Rome he was only a name, one among many commanders of legions.

Rome had garrisons to maintain in Africa and in Spain ; all down the coast of the Adriatic and beyond into Palestine and Judea the power of Rome stretched and her army had to be looked after ; the whole of Spain was garrisoned, and the entire area of Gaul right up to, and indeed beyond, the Rhine.

Small wonder, with all this to supply, that the Quarter-master-General in Rome kept a minutely careful eye not only on every man, but on every animal, every pick and shovel even, that the Army owned. If an ox or a horse belonging to Rome had died, Rome wanted to know why ; if the legate in charge of a legion had exercised his powers and commandeered some more animals, Rome would probably approve his action in the end, but it would want to know his reasons first.

The boy knew nothing of this ; he only heard the cries and saw the four oxen in the bright sunlight ; and watched the middle rubble of the road being slowly and laboriously rolled down.

Beyond where the oxen were working, on that part of the middle rubble that had been rolled until it was ready for the next and final step, there were again three legionaries and three auxiliaries at work.

This was craftsman's stuff again, mason's work. These men were laying the actual surface of the road, crowning all that had been done beneath and preparing the face which was to stand up to wind and weather, to sandalled foot or iron-shod wheel, and proudly to proclaim ROME to the world, for two thousand years.

This top to the road was made of flat stone slabs very carefully fitted ; and the boy noticed that when two stones had been laid close together, the legionary doing the work dug a small iron blade into a heap of something on a board at his side and worked it into the crack between the stones.

Speculate as he might the boy could not guess what this particular operation was. He had never even heard of cement, and knew neither the nature of it nor the use. He gave up wondering about that and moved a little farther on to the finished part of the road, along which a convoy of ox-drawn wains had just arrived, laden with fresh material.

Six miles they had come, though the boy did not know this, from a quarry in the next valley. It was impossible to tell from the appearance of the oxen how far they had travelled. There were three of them to each wain, and the journey had taken three and a half hours. It would have taken the same teams the same time had they been lugging loads half the weight or twice as heavy. They went at the pace of an ox, never more, occasionally less; and they looked out on the world with large, patient eyes and thought the frenzied activities of man very foolish indeed.

When the drivers gave the long, wail-like ' who-o-o-o-o ', telling the teams to stop, and put the goad-sticks away, a fresh activity took place.

Here a group of about twelve auxiliaries were busy off-loading the stones into open wicker-work baskets and carrying them to where they were actually wanted in the construction work.

As he watched, the boy became aware of a different atmosphere here. Farther along, one of the mason legionaries had been whistling the latest marching song as he worked, and an auxiliary had hummed snatches of it with him; but here was neither whistling nor humming.

Here, at the back-breaking work of loading and carrying the big wicker-work baskets, there was a smouldering surliness.

The boy could have felt it even if he had not been able to understand the quick words and half-sentences that the auxiliaries passed to one another as they worked.

There wasn't a legionary in charge of them because there wasn't a legionary to spare. They were working under the direction of a typical Briton. He was as short and dark as the rest of them, but very long in the arm, very powerful and muscular across his shoulders. And he was a very discontented and angry man. As each basket was filled and then carried off by two auxiliaries he grumbled. He grumbled about the work, saying that the loads were too heavy; about the road, saying it was useless and a waste of time; about Rome, saying that she took everything and gave nothing.

And if the others working with him did not grumble as much, or as vocally, as he did, some of them at least had sympathy with what he said.

The boy was dismayed, listening to all this. Grumble at

35

Rome ? Why, it was like finding fault with your own mother and father, with the gods themselves.

He tried to ignore the mutinous remarks and to concentrate on the details he could see. The wicker-work baskets interested him because they were exactly like the ones the women made in the hamlet in the winter-time, and he himself had more than once helped to cut young withies from the sedge side for the purpose.

'*Don't carry it.*'

Two auxiliaries who had been bending to lift a load looked up sharply.

' Don't carry it,' the broad-shouldered man said again.

The other two were uncertain.

' But, Wilder——' one of them began.

' But nothing ! But, but, but. Bah ! you're like all the womenkind. Catch sight of a Roman helmet and all the sense goes out of your heads. Rome ! All Rome means for the likes of us is an animal's life carrying stones about. Let Rome build her own roads and carry her own stones. I won't.'

' Will you not, then ? '

The calm, level voice came from just behind the boy, and he jumped. He had been so absorbed in watching and listening to what went forward among the unloading team of auxiliaries that he had forgotten all else. He had not noticed that the Centurion had left the surveying instrument for a while and had taken a stroll along the line of work to see how things were going.

Mansuetus, the Centurion, was not altogether surprised to find trouble among the unloading gang. They weren't all his men really ; they didn't all even belong to his legion. In the old days, when he had first come on foreign service to Britain, the legions had never been mixed. The XXXth always was the XXXth and nothing else. Of course, you got shifted about a good deal and sometimes you were sent away

36

on detachment ; but wherever you went, whether you were building the amphitheatre at Verulamium, or the city walls at Eburacum, where the headquarters of Northern Command was, or the big arch over the Via Fossa leading out of Lindum Colonia, you were a bit of the XXXth, under your own officers ; and if you had any auxiliaries with you they would always be your own, as much a part of the Legion as you were yourself.

But in the last ten or fifteen years that had changed a lot. Especially in the road building and pioneer corps. Now auxiliaries were made up into 'special service sections' and didn't seem to belong to any particular legion. At least not to belong in the way in which Mansuetus understood belonging to a legion—to belong to it body and soul, to regard it as your mother and father ; your be-all and end-all ; your family and home ; your world.

Nowadays, when you got a pioneering job to do, you indented to Caerlon for a 'special service section' of auxiliaries and you had to take what they sent you.

And sometimes they were not of the right sort. . . .

All this went through the Centurion's mind quickly enough as he asked quietly :

' Will you not, then ? '

Wilder, standing with his back to the ox-cart, said nothing. He scowled and looked what he was—an angry and a dangerous man.

They faced one another : the tall man with the metal-work gleaming on his shoulders, and the short, dark man in his stained and worn leather jerkin ; and each was thinking hard.

The very gleam and glint of the polished body armour, the miniature silver eagle on the left breast with XXX stamped proudly below it ; these things Wilder hated. They stood for everything that irked him. They meant order and re-straint. He could see behind them the squares of every Roman

37

camp ; the carefully swept and tended space in front of the praetorium, even when the praetorium was only a hut ; the lists, the orders, the saluting ; the everlasting and all-embracing discipline. He hated it all. And he bitterly regretted the folly of enlisting in the auxiliaries. Once you were in, you were in ; they did what they liked with you. He hated Rome ; her arrogance and the unfairness. He hated now, this man who represented it all.

Mansuetus didn't hate the auxiliary. He was sorry about him.

It was forty years since Mansuetus had come to Britain. Forty long years ! Even to think of it made him feel old. He didn't believe there was anyone else working on the road job who was more than thirty years old, all told.

.   .   .   .   .

Forty years ago Mansuetus had been fifteen years old ; a man in the eyes of Rome, old enough to share her fortunes and help bear her burdens. On his fifteenth birthday he had been gazetted as a very junior officer into the famous XXXth —his father's Legion before him. His name had gone up in a long list hung on the walls of the basilica :

'*Mansuetus, son of Constantine, Roman citizen and servant of the State.*'

Then followed six months square-bashing at the Legion's depot just outside Rome, along the Via Campagna. This was tough work for a boy of fifteen because the XXXth always boasted that their officers were put through it harder than the ranks, and that there wasn't a thing a man in the ranks could do which the most junior officer couldn't as well.

It wasn't quite true, of course ; but the savage old drill-instructors along the Via Campagna did their best to make it so, and soon the boy's hands were raw with handling his gladium in the close-fighting drill, all according to the text-book ; to say nothing of the back-breaking pilum exercises—

38

and after an hour of that on the barrack square you felt exactly as though you had been stretched on the rack, and you couldn't sleep at night because the muscles of your back ached so.

And on top of it all—the marching !

They were never satisfied at the depot that you could march well enough. Never. The military tribune in charge of the barracks had retired from active service after fourteen years in Spain, and was all the more of a fire-eater on that account. He was a martinet on marching. In fact, all the young officers thought him more than a bit mad on the subject. It was under him, and under the grim necessity of those sixteen, eighteen, and even twenty-four mile daily marches, carrying 'full foreign marching kit', that Mansuetus learnt to look after his feet. And in his subsequent forty years of service he had never ceased to be grateful to the peppery old tribune who had so often cursed him up hill and down dale in the old days.

Six months of the Via Campagna saw the young officer leaner and tougher in body ; and in mind just beginning to realize that there was a great deal in the wide world to learn and to digest.

Then his posting order for abroad came.

Normally he would not have been sent until he was sixteen and a half ; but the XXXth was short of young officers, and when he was six months short of the proper foreign service age his name went up.

Britain !

It might have been to Africa, because the XXXth was split in two. Half the infantry and all the cavalry were south, doing coastal patrol work—dull routine stuff compared to fighting—in the Mediterranean Command ; and the rest of the Legion was away up north in that mythical place which nobody seemed to want to be posted to : Britain.

' Take plenty of warm clothes.'

' Mind the icicles.'

' You won't get a bath till you come back.'

' Bring back a bear or two.'

All the old cracks were made at his expense, especially at his farewell party.

And the next morning he left, second in command of a batch of recruits, and in company with a similar batch going to the IXth at Lindum.

When the short, brassy bugles were sounding the ' fall-in ' for the first morning parade, they swung out of the big barrack gates and headed north along the Via Campagna, leaving Rome behind them.

Fourteen weeks it took them, to the day. Of course there was none of your twenty-four mile a day stuff now. That belonged to the mad business of intensive training. Once you were out of that and really in the Army, Rome used you very differently. You were precious material now and she husbanded you.

Twelve miles a day was the marching rule of the Imperial Army. Neither more nor less. And most of that was done before the ninth hour, so that even in the places where there wasn't a regular marching camp to end up at, you had plenty of time to get everything shipshape and four-square for the night.

Those fourteen weeks had opened the young officer's eyes all right. Until then he had read and been told and imagined ; now he saw.

Mile after mile ; day after day ; the countryside changing ; the horizon altering ; the skies and the people under them differing ; but one thing constant and unchanged all the time : Rome.

Wherever they camped for the night, the Imperial Army Service Corps somehow knew of them and were ready with their rations ; the post travelled faster than they did, and the

Post Office did not forget them. At three places across Gaul and, lastly, at the very port of embarkation, letters from home were waiting for them when they arrived. Every day on the interminable, long, straight roads they met signs of the Imperial Power : pioneer sections repairing the road itself ; engineers building a bridge or an aqueduct ; the fast-moving, horse-drawn chariots of the Post Office ; some important official with his retinue. The business of Rome filled the roads of the world, and wherever they went the silver eagle of the XXXth was saluted with respect.

And then there had been the long ship and the sea.

Until that moment young Mansuetus had never been on shipboard ; but he reported to the embarkation officer on the quayside (a hard-bitten old regular who had seen so many troops go across to Britain that he had long since lost count of them), and marched his men on board as though he knew all about it.

Or so he thought, until the rasping voice of the E.O. floated up in angry query.

'What in Hades are your men carrying their pilae for ?'

Mansuetus had forgotten that each man should have given up his pilum to the baggage sergeant, who would issue them again on disembarking.

'D'you think you're going to fight a campaign on board ship ? Don't they teach you young officers *anything* in Rome nowadays ?'

Mansuetus went white with rage ; but he said nothing. The E.O. was two ranks above him, so he shut his mouth tight and said nothing. But the impropriety of it offended and infuriated him. For one officer to speak to another thus, in public, in front of his men !

But in an hour's time the insult was forgotten. And, *pro tem*, everything else too. A stiff south-west wind, half a gale, was blowing up the narrow sea, and when they stood out clear of the coast of Gaul, their ship did things the young officer would not have believed possible.

And not only the ship but his own inside. Young Mansuetus had been desperately and violently sea-sick. For four hours at least he had not really cared whether the transport ever reached Britain, or sank on the way. He didn't care about the XXXth; or the Eagles; or even Rome itself. He cared for nothing but the misery of his poor inside.

And all the time the men who manned the ship, Britons, ran barefooted about the crowded deck; shouted a quick unintelligible word or two to each other; laughed occasionally; and generally didn't seem to mind in the least that the ship stood on her head every fourth minute or so, and that the sea reared up over them in threatening mountains.

This was the first time he had ever seen any Britons, and they impressed him.

Gradually they ran under the lee of the land a little and the wind and the sea abated. Mansuetus found that his acutest misery had passed and he began to notice things again. By this time it was dark (they had had to come out of Bononia on the late afternoon tide) and it was cold. There was no moon and Mansuetus could have sworn that the light he found himself staring at was no star; and yet what else?

'Dubris,' said an old hand standing on the deck by him.

Mansuetus turned in query.

'Dubris,' the man who had been to Britain before repeated; 'where we land if the wind is this way. They put in at Lemanis, Dubris, or Rutupiae according to wind and tide. All three of these are all right. If you're very unlucky you get carried round the point of Kantium and they shove you ashore at a god-forsaken spot called Regulbium where there's nothing but the barracks. But we're all right tonight; Dubris isn't at all bad.'

'And the light we can see?'

'That's the Pharos. Built on top of the cliffs. Agricola had it done the first year he came here. It's kept alight in hours of darkness all the year round. I call it *occulus Britanicus*. It gives me rather a friendly feeling every time I see it.'

'You've been here before?'

The other yawned. 'Many times. I'm always doing the journey. I'm bored to tears with it by now.' He held up a leather case stamped with the Imperial Eagle. 'I'm on special courier work between Britain and Rome. Of course, you get the best of everything on the journey—I mean, people make a fuss of you at the inns and so on; and I'd soon get the War Office down on them like a load of bricks if they didn't. But I get tired of the everlasting travelling.'

Mansuetus stared at the pharos, whose light was growing steadily larger as the ship drew nearer to the shore. A pharos, here, on the remote and almost mythical coasts of Britain! The fact had impressed him enormously.

.   .   .   .   .

Such had been the manner of his first coming to Britain forty years ago. And as chance fell out he had never been back to Rome.

It was normal to get home leave, even if you didn't get a posting, after five years of overseas service, but very often in a soldier's life the normal doesn't, or can't, happen; and on the first two occasions when a chance of leave occurred, Mansuetus couldn't take it.

After that he hadn't bothered.

He had fallen in love with the place by then, and it had become home to him. There were many like him; and at the War Office back in Rome they had a semi-affectionate, semi-scornful word for them.

'Here's another one,' they said in Records, receiving his request for permanent British Service, 'Mansuetus of the XXXth; he's become Britonicized.'

43

He had got to love the place and the people. It was a man's life : fighting and building ; a lot of building and a little fighting. A sense of making something all the time, and a spice of danger.

And, also, the fun of dealing with the Britons. Of trying to win them to Rome. Of catching them up and welding them into the greatest thing in the world—the universe of law, order, duty, and discipline which was the Imperial Army.

Not that they were all to be so won.

In Britain you were always in frontier conditions ; there was always danger. There was always the man who felt where the yoke rubbed him, and who could not get used to it. The man who looked at you with sullen and smouldering eyes.

As did the man who now refused to handle his load of stones ; and who might, if he wasn't dealt with properly and quickly, infect the rest of the unloading gang with his mood. . . .

' Why won't you carry the load ? ' he asked the mutinous Wilder. ' What's the matter ? '

The Briton said nothing ; but the boy, watching fascinated, saw him swallow hard.

' Aren't you an auxiliary of the Imperial Army ? ' The Centurion's voice had hardened a little.

' I am. More fool me.'

' Who forced you to become one, then ? '

' Mead. I was dead drunk in Atrebatum one night, or they'd never have got me in this outfit, don't you worry.'

' But you *are* in.'

' Yes. I'm in.'

' What are you, a seven-year or a fourteen-year man ? '

' Seven. I wasn't as drunk as all that.'

' How long have you done ? '

' Two years and three months.'

44

'And you've had your pay and rations regularly all that time?'

It was safe enough to ask *that* question, for wherever her soldiers were, in the heart of the Great City itself or scattered on the loneliest outpost of her empire, Rome never let them go unpaid or unfed.

'I've been fed and paid.'

'Then you must work for it.'

Wilder said nothing to that; but the boy noticed that he reached back one hand and rested it on the ox-cart behind him.

'Listen, you young fool,' Mansuetus went on, 'I've only to tell my sergeant to clap you under a guard and march you back to Isca and you would be given three months in the military prison there for this; don't you realize that?'

All pretence at the unloading work had been given up now, and the whole gang of auxiliaries was pressing round. The boy was standing with them, pushing his way to the front so that he might miss nothing.

Young as he was, he knew quite certainly that the climax of the thing had been reached. It was will against will now; authority against chaos.

And every other man there knew the same. They stood waiting, in complete silence, to see what the outcome would be. The old idea that some day the vast imperial machine would begin to show a crack was never altogether absent from the back of their minds. . . .

They all knew that what the Roman officer was saying was perfectly true. You couldn't refuse to obey an order in the Imperial Army and get away with it. Every legion dealt with its own offenders and had its own military prison. That of the XXXth was at what the Romans called Isca (the Britons knew it as Caerlon), and if Wilder was unlucky enough to get sent there he would most certainly regret it. The prison at Isca had a most unsavoury reputation.

45

Nobody knew all that better than Wilder, and his dark eyes smouldered sullenly because of the knowledge.

The boy noticed the fingers of the man's hand beginning to tighten round a good-sized, sharp piece of stone that he could feel on the ox-cart behind him. And seeing this the boy's heart dilated for a moment with fear : ' *he's going to hit the Centurion,*' he thought.

And Mansuetus, although he couldn't see the other man's fingers, thought the same thing. He was watching the Briton's eyes ; and the eyes of your friend or your enemy tell you a lot.

For perhaps four seconds nobody spoke, and the Centurion knew that the crisis was here. Strike a spark in this atmosphere and there would be an explosion.

' Why won't you carry the load ? ' he asked quietly. ' Is it too heavy ? '

' Too heavy for me, anyway,' Wilder answered grudgingly.

It was not really what he wanted to say ; but it was precisely and exactly what the Centurion wanted to hear. The talk was down to stones again now. Something practical. Something they all knew and understood.

He turned and looked at the basket laden with stone which was resting on the ground, the cause of all the commotion.

Everyone else turned and looked at it as well, including the boy.

' Throw another stone in,' Mansuetus ordered.

An auxiliary standing nearby hesitated for a moment and then silently did as he was told, and pitched a fair-sized stone on top of the already full basket.

His action was watched in silence.

' Stand clear,' Mansuetus ordered cheerfully, ' and let us see whether what is too heavy for a couple of you Britons can be managed by a single Roman.'

The little crowd moved slightly so as to let him get to the basket. He didn't like doing any heavy work with his helmet on, so he unbuckled the strap beneath his chin and swept the whole thing off.

'Hold this,' he said, hardly looking where he held it forth, and the boy found himself with a Roman helmet in his hand.

By chance he had been standing next to the laden basket, and when the crowd shifted to let the officer come near, eel-like, limpet-like, boy-like, he still managed to stay there ; so that when the Centurion said, ' *Hold this* ', there he was !

You could see, now his helmet was off, that there was more than a handful of grey in the Roman's hair. But grey hair or no, he looked at that moment like a very god to the boy.

He didn't feel like a god. He felt very different. He felt fifty-five years old and suddenly only too conscious of the fact that, however fit you are, the heart and lungs and muscles won't do the things for you at fifty-five that they would at twenty-five. A nice fool he'd look if he couldn't shift the thing after all ; and a nice fool he would make Rome and Roman authority look, too. He had a horrible moment of being tempted to think that he would have done better after all too stick to the text-book and have the stupid auxiliary clapped into Isca jail for three months, and settle the whole thing that way. Only that way wouldn't really settle anything, he knew in his heart of hearts ; and this just might. . . .

Bending, he laid hold of the two handles of the wicker-work basket, one on either side.

Then setting his teeth, he lifted.

It was a reasonable load for two men, but a most damnable and unfair load for one.

But then this one particular man, in these particular circumstances, just *had* to lift it.

And he did.

He thought something was going to snap somewhere, especially among the small muscles of his back, but he lifted

47

and went on lifting. The heavy basket came well clear of the ground ; and the boy could easily have broken into a cheer.

The Centurion held the basket there for a moment without moving, not really because he wanted to show off, although it looked a bit like it ; but because he was wondering whether he had sufficient strength left to accomplish the next part of it.

'Well, enough strength or not,' he told himself grimly, 'I've got to do it. Just *got* to. For Rome's sake. So here goes.'

Slowly but steadily, he began to carry the basket across the distance, fifty long paces maybe, that separated him from the spot where the stones had to be tipped out.

Before half the distance was covered his heart was pumping hard and the blood drumming in his ears. But he kept on ; he made himself keep on ; and for the last fifteen paces it was grim work.

He made it—just.

He made it, and lowered the heavy load carefully to the ground. The auxiliaries had followed and were standing round. He smiled cheerfully at them as he straightened up.

'There you are, lads,' he said. 'If an old man like me can do the job, two of you ought to be able to tackle it without too much grumbling. Come on now, get moving with it.'

There was a quick ripple of grudging laughter, a jest or two from one Briton to another, and everybody, the boy included, knew that the crisis was over.

The auxiliaries turned and trooped back to work, Wilder with them. But the boy caught sight of Wilder's face and he thought : 'It isn't all over with him. He's angry, like a cornered fox, and when he gets a chance he'll bite.'

The Centurion watched them going back to work, but he did not see the look on Wilder's face. He was relieved to get the thing over.

'I don't suppose that was strictly in accordance with

48

regulations,' he thought, ' but then the people who draw up the regulations sit on their backsides in Rome and don't come to Britain. If ever we fail to keep this part of the Empire, that will be the cause of it.'

Aloud he called : ' Where's my helmet ? '

' Here, sir.'

The boy had been carrying the metal helmet as carefully as though it had been a handful of eggs, taking especial pains not to crush or harm the short plume on top of it.

The Centurion took it, and was aware of the boy for the first time.

' Hallo,' he said, ' who are you ? A camp follower ? '

The boy nodded. Speech was beyond him. When he had set out that morning from the hamlet, determined to see this activity of which he had heard rumour, he had imagined a good deal ; but it had never entered his wildest dreams that he would be, as it were, caught up in the thing and actually speaking to a Roman centurion.

Mansuetus smiled at him. British boys often hung about the Imperial Army, and he always encouraged them. He made friends of them for Rome's sake. The more friends Rome had the better. Mansuetus always hoped that every British boy he took some notice of and cracked a joke with would, in time, grow into an ardent and Romanized auxiliary.

' You're lucky you don't have to wear a thing like this,' he said, putting on his helmet again and adjusting it in position.

The boy laughed at what he recognized as an intentionally idiotic remark. *Lucky* NOT *to be wearing the gleaming plumed helmet of a Roman Centurion*—what a thing to say.

But in a sense Mansuetus meant it. The helmet was one of the new pattern which the wiseacres of the War Office in Rome had thought up only a year before. The old sort, which had remained unchanged, to the Centurion's own knowledge, for at least thirty-five years, had no buckle

49

under the chin, but a small adjustment for the strap close to the left ear.

'Why they wanted to change the thing, I can't imagine,' Mansuetus grumbled, tugging at his chin-strap. 'This new metal buckle under the point of the chin is most fiendishly uncomfortable.'

As he adjusted the strap, the boy noticed for the first time a ring glinting on a finger of his left hand. Gold. The centurions of Rome even had gold on their fingers !

Mansuetus shot a sideways look at him and smiled.

'You interested in roads ?' he asked.

The boy, all but trotting to keep pace with the long legs, nodded almost ecstatically. Interested in roads ? What a question ! Of course he was interested in roads ; and in life ; in the business of being alive and alert on that windy March day ; in seeing, hearing, and touching Rome. It all added up to something so miraculously exciting that the intense pleasure of it hurt him.

They had made their way back along the side of the stream and by now had reached the point where he had first seen the Centurion.

'Ever seen the line of one laid out ?'

The boy shook his head. 'No, no, I have seen nothing till this, today.'

'Ah, you should follow the Eagles ! You'll see the world right enough then. The Senate pays you and feeds you and moves you about in every known quarter of the world. And some that aren't known, believe me. *Mind that groma !*'

This last injunction was called out in Latin to the young auxiliary who, in the absence of the Centurion, had been using the surveying instrument ; but it was called out too late. The young man had swung round quickly with a staff in his hand, and had accidentally brought it smartly against the central upright of the groma.

The whole thing swayed perilously and the Centurion, letting out a good round Roman oath, snatched at it just in time to stop it from going flying.

There was an instantaneous glint of gold in the March sunshine and the boy saw the man's ring shoot off his finger and go straight into the stream.

The water ran boisterously, creaming into white foam over the many stones, but crystal clear. It wasn't deep, perhaps four feet at the most, and the bottom at that particular spot was sandy. The boy could actually see the gold ring lying on the sandy bottom ; and almost before anyone else had quite realized what had happened, he had slipped off the old skin that was his only covering and gone naked in.

The water was cold ; cold enough to take his breath away ; but he took in a deep gulp of air, pinched his nose with thumb and forefinger of his left hand, and ducked his head underneath with his eyes wide open.

In less than a minute he was out again on the bank, triumphant. The wind felt twice as cold now ; but he hardly noticed it. He held out his right hand. The water streamed and glistened away from it in the March sunshine ; and in the upturned palm lay the ring.

The Centurion laughed.

' By Jupiter ! That was smartly done. I hardly knew I had lost the thing. It's been loose these six months. Good boy, I wouldn't have lost that for a fortune.'

The air was suddenly alive with the shrill, unmelodious notes of a pipe which the sergeant of cooks was blowing from beside the field ovens.

The thin notes had hardly had time to crawl up into the air before orders were being shouted ; and just as quickly as the orders reached them, men everywhere, both legionaries and auxiliaries, were leaving their work, putting down picks, baskets, and spades in obedience to the welcome sound.

'The sixth hour,' the Centurion said, watching them with a smile on his face. 'You'd almost think they'd heard it before, wouldn't you? Well, I like to see men hungry. Work 'em hard and feed 'em well. That's the way to do it.'

He turned and looked at the boy.

"What about you? Have you got anything to eat?'

The boy shook his head. When he had left that morning to seek adventure he had not made provision for food. He had not even thought about food. Such was not youth's way.

'Well, you had better take a bite with me. You rescued my ring and the least I can do is to give you a mouthful of food.'

They walked together to where the Centurion's tiny, one-man tent of hide had already been pitched and a man was waiting with an earthenware bowl of hot stuff.

'Larks' tongues and quails again, Camus?' the Centurion asked.

'That's right, sir,' the man laughed. 'It'll be nightingales tomorrow, I shouldn't wonder.'

'Bring a bit more if you can. I've a visitor.'

'I'll scrape the pot, sir, and see what we can do.'

'Hot pease-pudding,' the Centurion said, staring at the steaming mass on the platter. 'It's all the Imperial Army cooks can think of, apparently, in Britain. I must have eaten cart-loads of it in my time. Well, it's better than nothing, I suppose.'

He dodged into his tent and came out again with two short bits of wood, widened and slightly hollowed at the end.

'Issue spoons,' he said. ' " Spoon, wooden, officer, for the use of," that's how the office-bound wonders in the Q.M.'s department describe them. You wouldn't know about that, of course. If you are of centurion rank you get two—but you don't get twice as much food, believe me. Here, catch.'

He threw one of the spoons to the boy, who caught it

dexterously. He had never seen one before. At home he ate with his fingers, supplemented, when necessary, by a piece of stick picked from the ground.

He was hungry and the pease-pudding smelt good.

'But first—' the Roman said, and took hold of the boy's shoulders from behind, one strong hand on each, turning him to face the sun.

The boy turned as the hands directed him, but wondered what it was all about.

'It's the sixth hour; and at the sixth hour in this country, Britain, your country, *our* country, the sun is always in the same spot. Did you know that? Now turn this way, sinister-wards, so—' and he made the boy swing through a half-turn to the left '—and where do you think we are facing now?'

The boy thought hard; he had a good sense of direction; there was something inside his head which told him where he had come from and how to get back there.

'Wanna's Ford,' he replied with a deal of assurance in his voice.

The man laughed. 'Maybe. You'd know all about that, I daresay. But somewhere beyond Wanna's Ford, my young friend—Rome.'

'Rome!'

'Ay. I've done this every midday for forty years. Turned to the left of the sun and thought for five long breaths.'

Forty years! the boy thought; it was difficult to imagine such a time.

The pease-pudding was savoury and hot. The Centurion divided it in two, and the boy fairly gulped his down; and just as they were finishing the last of it, the assistant cook came along with a second helping and some dark rye bread, and they ate all that up, too; and the boy felt warm inside and well-fed.

Looking about him, he saw that the legionaries and the

auxiliaries ate separately, each group clustered round its own camp. The two cooks, having finished dishing out the food, were sitting together eating in front of the low humps of field-kitchens which looked like beehives. Every now and again a man would get up and take his leather water-bottle to the stream to fill it.

'How long do they eat for?' he asked.

'An hour. From the sixth to the seventh hour, that's the regulation in Britain. On what the War Office calls "foreign service, north". In Gaul and Rome itself it's different, of course. You won't get anybody there to do anything between the sixth and the ninth. The siesta, we call it.'

The word meant nothing to the boy. He was trying to picture Rome in his mind.

'Rome. Is it hot?' he asked.

'Hotter than here. But this suits me. I don't mind your grey skies and your wet days. All the old tribunes and prefects who retire to Aqua Sulis and spend half their time every day in the Baths there are always grumbling about the climate; but I'd sooner be here than Africa any day.'

'Africa? Is that somewhere? Have you been there as well?'

The man laughed. 'No. I haven't. So maybe I'm not a good judge after all. I've been nowhere for forty years but Britain. And I've been all over that.'

'It's a long time.'

'Ay, ay. It is. Too long. *Ehu, labuntur fugaces anni.* That's Horace. He lived the best part of two hundred years ago, when Augustus was Emperor and the Marcellan theatre was built in Rome. A great-great-great-grandfather of mine was the chief architect for it. I've got a book of Horace's *Odes* with me in the tent now. I always take it with me wherever I go. Of course, Caesar's *De Bello Gallico* is a text-book for all officers, but that's shop. Horace is pleasure.

And sometimes pain too. But that's the way things go. Things that you like and things that hurt you are often mixed up a bit ; have you found that ? '

' Ai, ai, ai.' The boy nodded, and said his swift agreement softly under his breath. It was so. You could be so happy that it hurt. The very miracle of being alive and of having the whole wide world spread out before you in shining new colours could bring a catch to your throat. It was so. And it was clever of the man to know it.

' Things are very different now,' the man was saying. ' When I first came here I was only a kid. The youngest officer in the Legion. Too young, actually, according to the regulations, to come on foreign service, north ; but I wangled that. I was sent to Isca, Caerlon *you* call it, where the Second has been for long enough now. My Legion, the XXXth, had just gone there to share barracks with them.'

' How many legions are there altogether ? '

' Ye gods, what a question ! How many legions ? Let me think ; I never see an Imperial Army List now ; you don't unless you're in Rome. There must be a hundred at least ; plus all sorts of odds and ends of specialist troops, of course.'

' A hundred legions ! And in each legion how many men ? '

' Five thousand, one hundred and twenty-four infantry, one hundred and thirty-two scouts—if you're up to strength, that is, which somehow you never are. The War Office is always niggardly about sending men to Britain. I ought to have fifteen legionaries on this job, but I've only ten.'

The boy was struggling in his mind with the vaster figures *...five thousand, one hundred and twenty-four....* Five thousand ; it meant nothing to him ; it was too big ; he had never seen five thousand of anything in his life.

' How many legions are there in Britain ? ' he asked.

'Ah, that's something I do know,' the man said promptly. 'Five. The Second and the Thirtieth at Isca; the Fourth at Eburacum—they've been up there almost as long as the Second have been at Isca—the Twentieth at Deva; and the Sixth, the Dainty Sixth, at Lindum. But, of course, now we've all got half our strength up at the Wall.'

'The Wall?'

'Ah, you Britons! you don't know what's going on round your own homes. You don't know your own history. When Caesar came over to have a look round a hundred and eighty years ago he only brought two legions the first time. Of course, they were good ones; the Tenth, who are in Spain now, and the old Fighting Seventh. That was only ten thousand men. They had a few Balearic slingers as well and some bowmen from the south, and they made a landing all right; but most of the boats got smashed up by a high tide, and your chaps here fought like demons, and the plain truth of it is that the Tenth and the Seventh, good troops as they were, had to come away with a flea in their ears.'

The boy squirmed with excitement.

'Go on,' he said, 'go on.' He had known confused and vague accounts of all this since he was a child, but they had not seemed real as this talk seemed, from a man who belonged to the machine that had taken part in it.

The Centurion laughed.

'What happened then was that Caesar got a severe reprimand from Rome. He might be just about the best commander on the Imperial Army List, but his raid on Britain had been a failure. And an expensive failure, too. You can't shift even two legions about, especially overseas, for nothing. So they had him on the carpet at Rome and told him he must try again and do better next time. He spent a year building a fleet of flat-bottomed transports at Bolonia, and training four legions in special disembarking drill. When he came the next year he had with him the Tenth and the Seventh again, because they knew something of the conditions ; and two other legions. I forget exactly which. The Eighteenth and the Fourth, I think. And some cavalry. Two thousand of 'em this time. He'd learnt *that* lesson anyway. It was lack of cavalry that let him down the year before.

'I suppose with about twenty-two thousand men he reckoned he had enough.

'He landed all right, and established a good bridgehead. But I think the sea must be on good terms with you Britons, because once again there was a freak high tide and most of the ships got knocked about badly. It wasn't exactly a total failure this time, but Caesar had to call the thing off after two months ; and reading between the lines, I think he was pretty glad to get his troops back to Gaul. Didn't you know all that ? '

The boy shook his head. ' I have heard men talk in the ale-house,' he said.

' Ah, the ale-house. *In vino veritas !* You won't know what that means. And it isn't true, anyway. There's more nonsense talked over the wine-glasses than in a full session of the Senate ; and that's saying something.'

' And Caesar ? ' the boy asked.

' Caesar gave you tough nuts of Britons best. In any case, he was made Consul, as they called it then, five years after the Second Expeditionary Force business, and I suppose he had too much to think about then. And five years after that he was assassinated. By his best friend, a man called Brutus, in the Forum at Rome. So that was the end of Caesar. But he's still one of the great names, in the Imperial Army, at any rate. After he had gone we didn't worry about Britain for nearly a hundred years. We had other things to think about. Rome was growing and changing. We got an Emperor in that time ; and it wasn't until the time of the fourth Emperor, Claudius, that the War Office took the Invasion of Britain plan out of its pigeon-hole again and blew the dust of nearly a hundred years off it.

' And this time they did things in style. I suppose Claudius studied the official reports of Caesar's two efforts and made up his mind to profit by previous mistakes.

' He put Plautius in charge. He wasn't anything like as good a general as Caesar, but he was competent. You don't become a general in the Imperial Army unless you are at least that. This time they made up an Expeditionary Force of thirty legions.'

' Thirty legions ! '

' No less. One hundred and fifty thousand infantry, and brought them over in the gods alone know how many flat-bottomed boats from Bolonia.

' Your chaps couldn't do much against thirty trained legions, at least not in the south, and that's how Britain became part of Rome.

' Of course, there were ups and downs. There was the Boudicca business in which the Ninth, the unlucky Ninth, got virtually wiped out and had to be completely re-formed ; and there were other scraps at various times. Things were really a bit unsettled until Agricola came and squared them up. Look—' he touched the boy on the arm and pointed in front of them.

Here, on a flat piece of ground by the side of the road construction works, about a dozen men, legionaries and auxiliaries mixed, were kicking a ball about. It was made of hide stuffed with straw and tied up, and two sticks had been set up in the ground a couple of yards apart, to serve as a goal at which the ball had to be kicked.

Legionaries and auxiliaries, Romans and Britons, were all happily mixed up in the free and easy game.

' *There's* Agricola for you,' the man went on. ' " You

aren't two nations," he used to say, " but one. You've got to get together and act as one. Learn their language and their jokes. Learn their games and play with 'em. And if you promise 'em anything, for Jupiter's sake stick to it." He had a special message like that written in the front of every soldier's pay-book.

' Added to which, he was the finest soldier the Imperial Army has ever had here, not even excepting Caesar.

' As soon as he came he saw that to be safe we must hold the north. It was no good pushing half-way up the island as far as Natae or Lindum, and stopping there with a perpetual threat from beyond. He saw that we must get the whole of Caledonia, and he very nearly did it. In fact he did do it for all practical purposes, right up to the high hills anyway, and no one in his senses would want to go campaigning in them. The poor old Ninth got a terrible mauling up there. It hadn't very long been re-formed after the first disaster, and Agricola took it up north with him from Lindum to blood the young soldiers and let the Legion see real active-service conditions. They got surprised in the night by some of your chaps and panicked in the camp, and in the morning there was very little left of the unlucky Ninth again.

' Oh, Agricola knew what he was doing all right ! The men fairly worshipped him, and the Britons used to turn out and cheer him like mad. And it takes something to make you British cheer.

' He wanted to take a force across to Hibernia in the west and add that to the Province. He could have done it easily ; the whole army was convinced of that. Two legions, or three at the outside, would have been enough ; but Rome wouldn't let him have them. There was an economy wave on at the Treasury, and they grudged him every man and animal he had up here.

' So Rome never got Hibernia and one day she will rue it.'

The boy's eyes were fixed on the game of kick-ball, a game such as he himself played with the other youths of the hamlet on any level bit of pasture land, but his mind was far away. His thoughts were running riot, ranging all over the wide world with the victorious eagles of the legions. He sat hugging his knees, his chin resting on them, and the pictures running like a film in his mind.

'And this man Agricola, is he here now?' he asked at length.

'Jupiter, no! He'd be a patriarch of eighty-four or five now if he was still alive. He was recalled from Britain the very year I came here.'

'Forty years ago!'

'Forty years ago. And he left his stamp on it for most of that time. General Hadrian's the Officer Commanding in Britain now. *He's* all right. He believes, as Agricola did, that the one thing we must do is to secure the north. That's why he's building the Wall.'

'A wall?' It didn't seem a very impressive undertaking to the boy. He knew walls. In the hamlet, although his own house and twenty others were made of wattle and daub, there were not less than six buildings with walls made of clay burnt into solid, square shapes.

The Centurion laughed, detecting the note of disappointment in the boy's voice.

'Ah, my young British friend, and how long do you think a wall might be?'

'It could be as long as six men are high,' the boy said after reflection. 'Or perhaps ten,' he added recklessly.

'Could it now? Then see how Rome does things. Listen. Hadrian's Wall is to be seventy-three miles long; seventy-three miles, boy.'

The boy shook his head.

'Seventy-three *miles*? Of one wall?' he repeated incredulously.

'Of one wall. Three tall men high. That's the way it's planned. An engineer officer from the Second up there on detachment was telling me about it. Seventy-three miles right across the island from Segedunum on the east coast across to the other sea. There are going to be fifteen fixed forts in it, and a permanent garrison of a legion and a half. A double ditch and a rampart all the way with theatres, shops, and Jupiter knows what for the troops. Well, I don't mind about those. The High Command has gone mad about supplying all that sort of thing these days. We're getting soft. You can keep all that as far as I'm concerned. But eighteen feet of masonry seventy-three miles long—that's something worth building. That's a Roman job. I would dearly love to be up there on it.'

'How is it you are not?'

The Centurion touched his grey hairs and laughed a little ruefully.

'What is it you Britons say? *Youth will be served*, isn't it? It's the cruellest sentence in the world ; and, unfortunately, the truest. General Hadrian doesn't want men of fifty-five. He reckons that any man over forty is getting old. He wants men of twenty and twenty-five. So I'm left to build roads in the soft south.'

The boy ran his eyes again over the vastness of the construction work in that small valley.

'But a road,' he said, ' that's a very wonderful thing.'

'It is. It is. Rome would be nothing without her roads. The roads *are* Rome. I got put on to road-making the second year I was here. The regular Assistant Surveying-Officer of the Legion went sick, and because I had learnt a little about land measurement at school, I was pushed into the job. And I've been at it ever since. I must have built more roads in Britain than any other officer in the Imperial Army. That's what they call me in the Legion now : Old Mansuetus, the road-maker.'

61

' And this road here ? '

' Nothing. Except that no road is nothing. At least no Roman road is nothing. Not if I make it, anyway. All the work has to be up to standard and specification. Not that the Inspector General worries much about me ; he knows I'll do the thing right. But I mean this road isn't an important one. Only a branch to make it easier to get the farm produce down to Isca—Isca Dumoniorum, that is, not Caerlon. That's where the Via Fossa starts and goes north-east like an arrow all the way to Lindum—ah, look ! '

There was some movement in the valley along the length of road already finished and a noise, half laughter, half cheering, went up from legionaries and auxiliaries combined.

Even the game of kick-ball was interrupted to watch the arrival of a hooded cart drawn by three horses harnessed unicorn fashion, two wheelers and a leader, and guarded by four legionaries marching two on either side.

' See their red sashes ? '

The boy nodded. Each soldier wore a red sash over his right shoulder and knotted on the left hip, and the cart itself had a broad red stripe over the centre of the covering hood.

' Fisci,' the Centurion explained. ' Pay-merchants. From the Paymaster General's department. There's a section at every legion headquarters. Pay-day's tomorrow, and every week, if the Legion has any of its men out on a job somewhere, the pay turns up in the special paymaster's van. The pay comes as regularly as the rations ; and that's what keeps the men in good heart.'

The same high-pitched, shrill whistle that had marked the beginning of the dinner-hour sounded again. There were good-natured grumblings and some laughter ; and one last, prodigious kick sent the ball of stuffed hide out of sight.

The Centurion watched it.

' I wouldn't be without that stuffed ball for anything,' he

said. ' Let the Briton have his game, play his game with him, and he's half yours already. I'm beginning to know my Briton.'

' I saw how you managed the man who said he wouldn't carry his load of stones.'

' Ah, Wilder ? He looks like being an Emperor's bad bargain. *He's* not half mine. And never will be, I'm afraid. He's one of the dangerous sort, I fear.'

The Centurion had risen now, and was walking back towards the site of the road-making, the boy by his side.

The officer had enjoyed the unusual dinner interlude ; he liked to talk to all sorts and conditions of people on his job ; it was part of its fascination for him. But now he was dismissing the boy from his mind, and beginning to think of the road and its problems again. He himself had not wanted to run it so close to the stream, but the Surveyor-in-Chief had ordered it so, and the Centurion had to obey ; but he could foresee all sorts of difficulties. Water was always difficult. . . .

He felt a tugging at his leather scabbard and looked round in some surprise.

The boy's eyes were shining and the words fairly tumbled out of his mouth.

The magnificent idea had been forming in his mind all that wonderful day, ever since he had first seen the field full of the might and majesty of Rome. Now at last he dared to put it into words and they fairly bubbled up in him.

' Let me come—with the auxiliaries—I want to join—to follow the Eagles.'

The officer halted and smiled down at him. He had made a convert, and an enthusiastic one. It was what he was always trying to do. Good ; good. But—

' Of what age are you ? ' he asked gently.

' Ten. Ten years. I'm a short-corn boy. I was born when there was no rain and the corn stood so short in the fields. Ten years ago.'

63

Ten—there was the rub. Rome wouldn't wear that. The central recruiting people in Rome hadn't been so strict years ago ; but things had tightened up a lot lately, and it was now laid down in black and white that no Briton was to be recruited into the auxiliaries until he was fourteen years old ; and then only with the consent of his parents.

He shook his head.

'Go back to Wanna's Ford, or wherever it is you live, boy,' he said, 'and look after the pigs, and come back again in four years' time.'

'Four years !' There was tragedy in the young voice.

'Ah, it will soon go. I may not be here. I won't be. But the legions and the auxiliaries will, don't you worry.'

'But I want to join now—*now*. I can leave home easily. I have brothers. If I am not there to tend the swine, another one will do it.'

'Ay, ay,' the big man laughed. 'Don't be impatient, son. Rome wasn't built in a day, that's how the old saying goes. You've got it all in front of you. Meanwhile—*hoc age*. Do the job on hand. My road for me, your pigs for you.'

He gave the boy a friendly, caressing cuff on the head and, shrugging his harness into a comfortable position on his shoulders, strode off in earnest this time.

The boy stood watching him. Something prickly and uncomfortable was at the back of his eyes. Not that he was really going to cry. Woman's stuff, that. And he was no woman ; but, but . . . the big men in their polished armour ; the sandalled feet tramp, tramp, tramping in unison along all the roads of the world ; the shouting and the laughter and the games ; the magic of it all ; the Eagles and Rome !

It was like a fever in his blood, and he could not tear himself away to start the long walk back over the hill and across another valley to Wanna's Ford.

The hamlet, the swineherd's hovel, and the pigs ; they had

been all his world and now they were nothing. They would be worse than nothing ; they would be a prison. He would go, he supposed, in the end. He would have to go. But not yet, not yet. . . .

But in the end he did not go. He couldn't. It was too fascinating. All that March afternoon the activity went on : organized, steady, efficient. It was like seeing the world built under your eyes. And always taking care to keep out of sight of the Centurion, who in any case was too busy to notice him, the boy managed not only to see most of what was going on, but in small ways to take part in it.

Lots of legionaries and auxiliaries were glad to have someone willing to run down to the stream with their leather water-bottles, fill them at the bubbling water and bring them dripping back ; and when one wheel of a bullock cart slipped into a deep rut and the whole heavily laden concern was like to go over, nobody minded how many extra pairs of hands hauled on the cords to right it again.

Unloading the stone as it arrived had been work for the auxiliaries only so far, but when this minor emergency arose, a legionary, a sergeant of engineers, was sent to deal with it.

He was in a bad temper, and when sergeants of the Imperial Army were bad-tempered they did not always treat the auxiliaries according to the official text-book for Handling the Troops, nor perhaps quite as the late General Agricola would have wished.

This particular sergeant had put in an application for posting back to Rome for urgent private reasons, and had just heard that it was refused. It seemed that the Senate and the Roman People badly needed the service of an experienced engineer sergeant in Britain, and really could not have cared less about his private domestic affairs.

Sergeant Nervus, therefore, was taking a dim view, at any rate temporarily, of all things British. He was already having trouble enough with the stream, which would certainly have to be piped and possibly even diverted ; and now to be taken away from that to deal with a semi-overturned bullock cart. . . .

' *Pull*, you spindle-legged lot of underfed nobodies ! ' he roared at them.

It was all rather silly, really, because the auxiliaries weren't at all spindle-legged ; at any rate Wilder certainly wasn't. The boy was pulling next to him, and could see the savage discontent in his face and hear the angry mutterings under his breath. And if anyone in the service of Rome was underfed, which they weren't, it was surely the fault of Rome itself and of nobody else !

These considerations, however, did not weigh with Sergeant Nervus.

' Mind those pole-bullocks,' he roared again ; ' we shall get a broken leg in a moment and that'll mean an inquiry.'

Like all soldiers, good or bad, the sergeant hated the thought of an inquiry.

' Lay hold of those ropes,' he shouted, ' and *pull* ! By the foot of Hercules, is that the best you can do ? Pull, you lot of lazy barbarians, *pull* ! '

General Agricola wouldn't have approved of the word ' barbarians ' one little bit. That wasn't the text-book way to foster the spirit of co-operation between the Imperial troops and the natives.

Not that the boy minded. The bad temper of the sergeant and the shouting and the oaths were all part of the fun for him. All varied, spicy tastes in the wonderful dish of life that the long March day had served up for him to enjoy.

He laid hold of the ropes and pulled with a will. He pulled until the palms of his hands were red and rough with pulling. And when (' ho, ho, ho, she's coming . . . hold her now . . . steady ') the heavy waggon was finally righted, he felt sure that it was largely his efforts that had done it.

After that he reverted to his self-imposed task of running down to the stream with the water-bottle of any auxiliary who looked in need of a drink.

He had just come back, for the third time, with the bottle of a short, thick-set man who seemed capable of drinking unlimited quantities of water, and was standing watching him drink, when a brassy bugle blared into the air.

Immediately work stopped and heads were raised expectantly.

'The eleventh hour,' the thirsty auxiliary said. 'We ought to be knocking off by rights ; but—'

A second cascade of bugle notes came tumbling after the first.

'Ah, I thought as much.

> " *Di-diddy, di-diddy, di-diddy-di-day,*
> Work on and like it ; Rome's busy today."

'That's the way it goes, sonny. Well, I don't know that you can blame old road-making Mansuetus ; he's got a ticklish job on here. But it won't please all of us, I can tell you.' He smiled at the boy and gave a jerk of his head which might, or might not, have indicated Wilder working some six yards away.

The boy was puzzled over the question of time.

'The eleventh hour ?' he queried. 'How's that ?'

'The Army's way of reckoning. Rome's way. They don't start the day at midnight like we do. Third cock-crow, that we call six, is where they begin. That's when the first relief of the guard is posted and the Army starts its day. And normally we work till the eleventh. That's what's laid down in the rules and regulations. Always provided that you're not in a jam, as we are today ; and then the Army can do what

67

it likes with you. We shall be lucky if we knock off in two hours' time, from what I can see of it. What a life, eh? Become an auxiliary and see the world—that's what they told me. Become an auxiliary and *make* the world, that's what it looks like to me.'

It turned out to be a pessimistic prophecy. One hour and one hour only ' over the regulations ' was worked, and then the bugle blew out again.

Road-making was over ; the day's work done ; now the Imperial Army must make ready for the night—all according to ritual, tradition, and the sacred text-book.

The boy watched it all, fascinated.

In the course of the day's work everything and everybody— men, materials, gear, and animals, had necessarily become spread out and in apparent confusion.

Now, in a few short moves, the Imperial Army, which loved orderliness and exactitude even more than any other army has ever done, was getting things straight again.

Picks and shovels were stacked in neat piles under the careful, counting eye of an N.C.O. Sacks and wicker-work baskets were similarly checked and stored. The groma and the surveying rods were jealously put away by the Sergeant Surveyor. Squad by squad the legionaries and auxiliaries were paraded and dismissed with a sharp word of command.

The boy saw that as the sergeant's word to dismiss rang out, the men of each squad all turned in one direction and paused for a moment before breaking rank. Like all the rest of the military ritual, it meant nothing to the watching youngster except that it was new and exciting and impressive. Had he known what this turn of the body at the end of each day's work meant, he would have been more impressed still.

At the end of every day, all over the Empire, wherever the Eagles were carried and the legions had marched, when the word ' dismiss ' was given—it might be by a Centurion to a full cohort on Ceremonial Parade, or by a rasp-voiced sergeant to a squad of working auxiliaries—the men made a turn to the right as a symbol that they acknowledged Rome to be the centre of the world.

Of course, to turn to the right wherever they happened to be couldn't actually bring everybody facing Rome ; the movement was symbolic only, so that from the farthest north, where Hadrian's wall was building in the mists, to Ctesiphon on the Tigris, or Sagrutum in Spain, men reminded themselves for one moment every day that civilization had a heart, which was Rome.

The boy knew nothing of this. He only saw the different squads of men break away ; and then under his fascinated eyes the camp life sprang into being.

There were three sets of tents. First, the small, solitary tent of the Centurion. Like all men on whom authority rests, he was condemned to be alone to a considerable extent. Then, a hundred yards away maybe, two tents for the Roman soldiers proper, the legionaries of the XXXth Legion. They were only a handful (eleven to be precise), but all was set out according to rule and regulation : the three sergeants in one tent, the eight legionaries in the other ; four clear feet between tents ; tent flaps not facing one another ; holding-ropes slackened slightly, because March dews are heavy.

A hundred yards farther away, at the far end of the whole encampment, were the six tents of the auxiliaries. They slept ten in a tent, and their tents were only three feet apart. Such were the regulations ; in such fashion were the tents pitched.

And now, outside each lot of tents the camp-fires began to smoke and glow and blaze in the gathering dusk.

The text-book said : ' one camp-fire per every dozen men, or part thereof,' so that the legionaries had one fire (a large one, the Sergeants saw to that), and the auxiliaries had five.

The boy watched all this with delight. Like every other dweller in the hamlet, he appreciated fire and felt worship for it in his heart. Fire was the powerful, friendly ally that made life possible.

In the middle of the camp the fiscal-wagon stood with its own small company of four and its own small fire. Evidently the pay-merchants believed in keeping themselves to themselves. At the back of the auxiliaries' tents, beyond the latrines, were the animal lines ; and these the boy inspected with the closest interest and attention.

The horses were tied at intervals to a long central rope fixed between two stout poles ; but each bullock was picketed separately. Two auxiliaries, the stable fatigue, were busy watering, feeding, or testing tethers and picket ropes, and generally looking after things.

Beyond this again a solitary, bored figure dressed in the full accoutrement of a legionary was standing ; the first sentry of the evening. For after nightfall no Roman camp was ever without its properly stationed sentry, who did duty for two hours at a time.

Not that the duty was taken very seriously here. You had to have a sentry, Imperial Army Regulations said so ; but there wasn't very much for him to do.

Up in the north, where the Wall was being built, or maybe in the middle of Wales it might be different. There might be something to look out for there ; but here in the civilized south, which was almost as Roman as Gaul . . . still, you had to have him ; it was automatic ; and there he was doing his two hours and counting himself lucky to be on the first shift, so that he would have the middle of the night for sleeping.

The boy saw all this ; understood, at any rate dimly, a great deal of it ; and marvelled exceedingly.

'Ai, ai, ai,' he said to himself softly, ' it is like a town, here in the field ; like a town.'

70

The fires were burning up now and the men were sitting round them cleaning their gear.

'Hey, you.'

The thirsty auxiliary whose water-bottle he had filled three times had caught sight of him in the shadows, and he called out again :

'Hey, little Hadrian.'

One or two laughed as he came rather uncertainly into the circle of the firelight, but nobody took much notice ; every camp was used to its hangers-on and followers.

'Come and sit down here, youngster, and help me clean this confounded stuff.'

The boy squatted down on his haunches, one of the circle round the fire now, and grateful to feel the warmth of it.

'Beech,' one auxiliary was saying. 'You can't beat it. Not to my way of thinking. I'll wager they haven't any wood as good in all Italy.'

'They've plenty of wine and big fat women,' another answered with a laugh, 'because I've been there.'

'Tell us.'

Any auxiliary who had been on service across the narrow sea, *trans Fretum Gallicum,* the Romans called it, was always sure of an audience.

'I was on attachment to the Second. The cavalry of the Second, that is, when they went to Gaul for a spell and then farther down into Italy itself.'

'What's it like ? '

'Ah,' the man spat into the fire, 'soldiering's soldiering the world over as far as I can see. But the wine's good. They've got vineyards for ever. And Rome ! ' he laughed. 'By the forked beard of Thor, you wouldn't believe Rome till you see it.'

'Britain will do for me,' the boy's own auxiliary said.

71

' I'll wager when you get to Rome you've only got to clean your gear twice as often.'

' That's about the size of it,' the other confessed. ' Still, if you've never seen the Imperial Guard come marching down what they call the Via Flaminia with all the bugles blowing. . . . Old road-making Mansuetus here, he'd have to buck his ideas up a bit in Rome, I can tell you.'

' Rub that hide scabbard up for me, boy.'

' Oil out of a neat's foot. That's what you want for a shine. You can't beat it for any sort of leather.'

' Well, I can—so ! ' The speaker spat hard and true on to the leather. ' Spit on it and polish it. Spit again and polish again. *That's* the way. You won't get any checks for dirty leather then.'

' We shall all be cleaning our leather up at the Wall shortly.'

' The Wall ? '

' This new job of the G.O.C.'s up in the north.'

' Ugh. The North ! Lindum's far enough north for me. And too far. Give me a nice office-cleaner's job at head-quarters at Caerlon and I'll be happy for ever.'

The boy, rubbing industriously at the leather gladium scabbard, was all ears. This was the talk to listen to. The talk of men who had proved themselves men up and down the world. Men who thought, not in terms of hamlets or hundreds, but of countries and continents. Magical, heady stuff.

Then an auxiliary who had been on a nocturnal prowl came back with a couple of conies, and when they had been dealt with faithfully in a pot over the fire (and to Hades with the Legion cooks !) the boy was given a mouthful in reward for his services.

And after there was singing.

Songs the boy knew, some of them. Old stuff, sung by the old men in the hamlet because they, when young, had heard it from the old men of their day. Ancient, dark songs of when the great forests were, and of when the Ice was. Fearful songs of when the wolves ran unchecked and the bears roamed. Old, happy songs of the cave and the raw bison-meat.

And there were newer songs, of course. The latest catch was always being brought over from Rome, two or three months late but nonetheless amusing for all that. Silly, sloppy songs about Lalage and Lesbia, Placidia and Patos.

And finally and inevitably there was the Legion's own marching song, the chant of the XXXth. Fine, resounding stuff that had gone with the marching feet from one end of the Empire to the other. And to sit there, hunched up, your legs tucked under you ; to feel the warmth of fire on your face ; to lift your eyes for a moment and catch a glimpse of the remote and uncaring stars above ; to hear round you the singing voices of men ; to feel about you the friendly pressure of companionship ; to smell the sweat and humanity of soldiers who had roamed the world—all this was potent magic indeed.

And above all, to listen to the talk, the everlasting, reminiscent, boasting, I've-seen-what-you-never-saw talk of soldiers was something never to be forgotten.

' Ay, ay—but when the Ninth were at Lindum——'

' The unlucky Ninth.'

' And that swine of a Centurion at Verulamium—remember ? '

Presently the moon came up, a large, bright, shining coin in the unclouded sky ; the fires began to flicker and to fade ; men yawned and stretched tired limbs, and it was time for bed.

' Don't be late in the morning.'

' Roll on my seven years ! '

' More road-making tomorrow.'

' Ay, the everlasting road ! '

They went off to the tents grumbling and laughing and

U T H—F   73

yawning and the boy was left alone, and unheeded, except that his auxiliary called out as an afterthought : ' Better not be there when the sergeant does last rounds.'

Not sure exactly what the words meant, but recognizing them as a warning, the boy left the fire and went fifty yards away into the shadows of three big elms.

He crouched there patiently. The night was turning much colder ; but that did not worry him unduly. He was nearly as impervious to weather as a dog is. It was inside him that his trouble lay. In his heart. He was unhappy. The Army had wrapped itself away for the night after its own fashions and traditions ; and it had no place for him. He was a camp-follower, nothing more. They would let him sit by the camp-fire for an hour or so, but that was only on sufferance ; and when that interlude was over the Army went its way, and for all the Army cared he could go whistling in the dark.

He cocked an eye at the sky. The moon was at the full and the night would be safe for travelling. Sometime during the darkness he would make the journey back to Wanna's Ford, and tomorrow when day came he would be ready to deal with the pigs again. The pigs !

But not yet ; not quite yet. The night stretched ahead of him ; he would wait a little yet, feast his eyes a little longer, if only on the sleeping, moon-silvered camp.

Presently he saw a solitary, burly figure walking briskly through the camp from one end to the other. It was the Sergeant of the day doing the traditional duty of ' last rounds '. Nothing to it. Not in a camp of this size, anyway. Different if you had a whole legion in the field . . . through the camp ; inspect the fires ; see that the tent flaps are pinned back open, unless it is raining hard ; a glance at the animals ; no lights anywhere ; no talking ; the Imperial Army wants you for hard work tomorrow, so it's your business to be fast asleep now. . . .

74

'Just as I'm going to be in a moment,' Sergeant Tullus promised himself, casting a last, quick, practised eye round and turning back towards his tent.

The boy watched him turn, walk back to the Sergeants' tent, and disappear inside.

'Last rounds' was evidently over; and the boy looked a little wistfully at the still considerable remains of the fire where he had been sitting. Although he was as impervious to the cold as any animal, yet like any animal he loved heat ... before he started out to Wanna's Ford it would be pleasant, very pleasant, to crouch by the red embers of the beech-wood fire for a space.

He rose, and, moving so quietly that only a wild, nocturnal thing could have heard him go, left the black shadows of the three big elms and made his way past the auxiliaries' tents towards the fire.

But he never got there.

The auxiliaries had six tents, and the boy was passing the outermost of them when he heard voices. One in particular. The angry Wilder's. He recognized it. And it was clear that Wilder was still angry. He was talking in that quick, urgent, compelling way which a man uses when his mind is set on some desperate adventure and he is urging his comrades to join him.

The voice was low, cautiously low; but the words were clear and unmistakable.

'There are only ten of them all told, or eleven.'

'And four more with the pay-wagon,' some unseen listener replied, not yet quite convinced.

'Fifteen! what's that? There are fifty of us; nearly sixty.'

The boy sank on one knee in the cold, wet dew of the meadow grass to eavesdrop better. His heart was thumping a little and he had to steady his breathing. . . .

75

'. . . if we could get the money,' a voice said, still a little uncertain but with greed creeping into it.

'If, if, if.' Wilder's voice was cutting with scorn. 'You mean *when*. *When* we get the money. What's to stop us? How long will it take to slit a Roman throat? And I'll give you the lead. When we've finished the pay-wagon guards, I'll start with that blasted Centurion. Will you have the guts to back me up then?'

There was a murmur of approval from the rest of the tent; the ugly, throaty murmur of men who are being persuaded into folly and worse.

It was enough for the boy; he knew that sound; it was a *pack* noise; the sort of noise that meant more to him even than actual speech. The snarl and the growl of the pack just before they sprang—and killed.

The boy got up and hesitated a moment in thought. Away to his right, in a coppice beyond the stream, an owl suddenly split the night's quiet with its derisive, menacing screech.

He shivered a little; he didn't like screech-owls.

Moving quickly, he glided away from the auxiliaries' tents towards the other end of the camp. It would have taken sharp eyes and ears to detect his going. Where there was any shadow he took advantage of it; where there was firm treading he used it; where there was danger of making a noise he avoided it. All this was instinctive, without the necessity of conscious thought.

When he got to the Centurion's tent there was hardly a gleam left in the ashes of the small camp-fire.

The tent flap was up (the Centurion's rank entitled him to have his tent flap down in any weather, but Mansuetus chose to set his men an example in small things) and through the opening the moonlight threw a triangle of silver light partly on the ground, partly on the truckle-bed on which the Centurion slept.

The boy hesitated for a moment and then darkened the silver triangle with his shadow.

'*Who's there?*'

Mansuetus had been asleep; but he slept lightly and he had the useful trick of waking instantly to full consciousness. He sat bolt upright, and his hand went out to where his gladium hung in its scabbard of hide.

'It's me. The boy from Wanna's Ford.'

The man's hand came slowly away from the gladium.

'So? What do you want, my little friend?'

'It's Wilder.'

'*Wilder?* That one. What of him?'

The boy told him, hurrying the words out, confusing them a bit in his excitement and repeating himself. But it was all clear enough for the Centurion, who listened in silent astonishment.

'Ye—Imperial—gods!' he said at length under his breath. 'So that's the way of it, eh? Mutiny. I ought to have put that gentleman under guard at once and had done with him. Tell me again, slowly.'

The boy told him; and once again the man listened, nodding; asking a question or two. He liked to know exactly what he had to deal with.

'All right,' he said at the end of the second telling. 'All right. Now I know. By Cerberus, the Tribune would have been pleased with me if I'd lost a week's pay for sixty men! You clear out of it, my little friend; there'll be trouble here before cockcrow. And '—the boy turned in the tent opening to listen to the last words—' boy from Wanna's Ford, don't think I shall forget this night's service, because I shan't. Now go. Into safety. Quick.'

The boy went back, as quickly and unobtrusively as he had come, to the black shadow of his three elm-trees.

'Never lie up under an ellum,' his father had told him

more than once. 'She's a tricky old tree at best of times. Holly's the driest, and oak's the friendliest, and thorn's the most ancientest.'

But he wasn't going to sleep there ; he was only crouching in the shadows, waiting and watching.

The camp lay quiet and peaceful still ; and it did not look as though anything was going to happen after all.

As he watched, the owl made its uncouth noise again and from farther away a night animal barked ; a dog-fox, he thought it was, rutting after a vixen.

A mass of black cloud that had been steadily advancing over the sky in a straight line began to obscure the moon, and the silver light faded from the elm branches, from the field, and from the camp.

Now you might have the best eyes in the world—and the boy's were as good as most—and you would find it difficult to see detail half a dozen yards away, or anything at all at twenty.

He cocked an appraising eye at the sky and judged that the darkness of the cloud would have passed in ten minutes or so. But meanwhile, dark it certainly was, and his keen eyes were but little use to him, so he stood up and leant his back against the bole of one of the elms and put all his senses into his straining eyes, expecting at any moment to hear the night's silence dramatically broken.

But nothing happened.

Were there some sounds ? It was not easy to tell, for the horses moved in their lines and the heavy bullocks breathed stertorously and shifted at their pickets.

'Wilder isn't going to do anything,' the boy thought, 'he daren't at the last moment. It was talk only—like the talk in the ale-house. And Rome ; Rome will be safe.'

The band of light which marked the bottom edge of the storm was increasing in width every moment now ; and the mass of dark cloud was moving across to the west just as though some gigantic, invisible hand was pushing it away from the face of the moon. Presently shadows began to show again ; tentative at first, then hardening and lastly attaining that particular intensity of darkness which only full moonlight can cause.

The camp was moon-silvered again, and sleeping and apparently quiet.

' Nothing's going to happen,' still thought the boy from Wanna's Ford ; and he did not have time to make up his mind whether he was glad or sorry, for the words were hardly formed in his brain when his eyes caught something.

Something *was* going to happen ; was happening now, in fact.

Figures were gliding through the moonlight.

They moved stealthily, only too well aware, now that they were committed to their folly, that their lives depended on getting the bloody work done quickly and quietly before Rome had woken to the realization of what was happening.

They came out of the dark shadows of the auxiliaries' tents and moved towards the middle of the camp where the pay-wagon stood with, as far as the boy could see, no guard on it at all now.

He counted the shapes as best he could. Fifteen certainly, and more that he could not entirely distinguish. Say twenty at the least, all told.

And the others would be waiting, he guessed, to see which way the thing went. . . .

Wilder was not without his followers, evidently.

And Rome ?

The boy strained his eyes anxiously and could see nothing to allay his growing fears.

It looked as though Rome slept.

Perhaps the Centurion had disbelieved him ; perhaps (the

thought assailed him for one wild confusing moment) the whole thing had been a dream, was still a dream, wasn't happening at all. . . .

' Now ! '

The single harsh word cut the silence startlingly.

It was Wilder's war cry. He was in the van of the mutineers and was delighted with the ease with which everything had gone so far. He was keeping a wary eye on the figure of the solitary sentry right at the other end of the camp. The man had his back turned to them and was gazing sleepily down the moonlit valley. Obviously he heard nothing and suspected nothing.

It even looked as though the guards who should by regulation be on watch by the pay-wagon had turned in for the night.

' More fools they,' Wilder thought, ' for they won't wake again in this world.'

When he judged himself to be near enough for the final pounce he let go that solitary eager word ' Now ! ', threw caution to the winds, and ran forward.

And on the very instant, just as though his exulting word had released a spring, the pay-wagon burst into life.

It was as though the vehicle itself had come alive.

The cloth sides of it were torn apart, the back flung open, and a dozen fully armed legionaries came clattering out.

The night was mad suddenly with oaths and shouting.

' Up the Thirtieth ! '

' Senatus populusque Romanus ! '

' Run for it, run for it ! '

Sword clashed murderously on sword ; an upraised shield glistened in the silver moonlight and a man shrieked in the long, two-seconds' agony of dying. . . .

The thing was dead almost before it came alive ; nipped in the bud ; the episode that was going to be called the Mutiny of the Auxiliaries near Dumonium in a host of official documents and references was really a very short-lived affair.

Two auxiliaries were killed on the spot; the rest gave up sheepishly almost at once, bitterly, but too late, regretting their folly; one was in flight with the Surveying Sergeant in murderous pursuit after him.

Wilder ran as he had not thought himself capable of running. If he was caught—he knew the answer to that one. If he could get away to the woods and the marshes there was a chance. . . . So he ran, making straight for the auxiliaries' tents, and beyond them for where three trees made a patch of protective shadow.

Standing there under the first elm, the boy watched them coming. The two men : one now frantic with fear, the other desperate to deal out death. Two figures which, for all their dreadful reality, seemed for a moment as though they might be unreal, something carved or scratched on a slab of stone.

But they were not carved or scratched on stone. They were real and moving. Coming straight towards him so fast that he had no time to make up his mind what to do. If he stuck out a foot, Wilder would come down like a pole-axed ox with the sergeant on top of him. If he didn't put out that tripping foot, if he did nothing, Wilder looked like getting away, for he was less laden than the Roman soldier and was gaining a lead. . . .

To put out that fatal foot or not ? The boy never knew what he would have done, because something settled the issue for him. Fate, if you like to call it that. Fate in the disguise of a tree-root sticking up dangerously above the ground, and invisible in the shadow of the elm above it.

Wilder, running faster than he had ever run before in his life, faster than he knew he *could* run, and almost beginning to hope that he could shake off his pursuer, hit that up-jutting lump of root good and hard.

He was going so fast that there was no question of stumbling or faltering. He went full length down on the ground with just the same headlong velocity he had been travelling at.

Almost at the horrified boy's feet.

And not two seconds later the Roman sergeant was on top of him ; the short, ugly blade of a gladium shone for one moment in a shaft of moonlight and then shone no longer.

Auxiliary Wilder, serving seven years with the Imperial Army as a self-enlisted man in the Pioneer and Road Construction Camps, would grumble no more now.

The Centurion was on the spot almost as soon as the Sergeant got to his feet.

'I've got him, sir,' the Surveying Sergeant said. 'By the Seven Hills, I never thought to see mutiny here in the south.'

The Centurion sighed. He could foresee the endless complications, the forms to be filled up, the reports to be written out, the inquiry and the investigation.

But suppose he hadn't been warned ; suppose the mutiny had succeeded even only for a time ; suppose the pay had been lost and Roman blood spilt ?

He couldn't bear to suppose it. Disgrace and ignominious dismissal from the Imperial Army would have been certain.

He caught sight of the boy standing motionless and wide-eyed in the shadows.

'The boy from Wanna's Ford,' the Roman Centurion said slowly. 'See this British brat here, Sergeant ? '

'Sir ? '

'He saved the day for us. You can count him one of the auxiliaries from now on. I'll fix it with Records somehow. Call him my personal servant, if you like.'

'Ay, ay, sir.'

The boy would have said something ; the words were bubbling up inside him ; the excitement and delight were so

enormous that he felt it must all burst out, when suddenly the night was filled with a brazen noise.

Something of the Army ? the boy wondered. Some bugle, or gong ? It grew louder and louder, sounding in his ears like a triumphant blaring of the Eagles' splendour. . . .

.   .   .   .   .

' Mus' Tom, Mus' Tom.'

Tom shook his head a little and climbed uncertainly back, out of the old oak-tree.

' Hallo,' he called. ' What's up ? '

' 'Tis old Liza beating the dinner-gong for elevenses. You can hear the old church clock a-striking the hour this mortal minute.'

Tom cocked his head and listened.

So you could, old Wilde was quite right . . . four, five, six, right up to eleven.

' Elevenses,' Liza was shouting from the house, ' and the Doctor will be wonderfully cross if you don't 'ave 'em, so come your ways in at once, my dear.'

Tom laughed. Elevenses sounded a jolly good idea. He was hungry and a bit tired somehow and curiously excited. . . .

He went his ways in and found a cup of steaming hot Bovril and a slice of plum-cake waiting.

Good old Liza !

PART TWO

BOOK-MAKERS

(Norman : A.D. 1085)

'Tom, Tom!'
 'Yes, Aunt Ella?'
 'Be a good boy and run down to see what's happened to Wilde, will you? He ought to have been back at two, and it's nearly half-past. You know where his cottage is, don't you?'
'Yes, rather.'
'*Tell him I'm waiting for the celery.*' This last was the agonized shriek of a housewife with four people coming to dinner that evening and none of the cooking or salad-making done yet.

It was no good asking any of the Mason children to go, for Jump was in bed with a sore throat and a temperature; and Eleanor and Jennifer were both going to a fancy dress party that evening. They had been shut up in their joint bedroom all the morning and had run upstairs again directly luncheon was over, with the strictest possible instructions that they were not available for any sort of duty or diversion for the next three hours.

Occasionally the door would be flung open and a despairing cry for help would come floating down the stairs such as :

'Mummy, Mummy, what's happened to the safety-pins?'

'Mums, could I possibly use that red velvet thing you got from the W.I. jumble sale as a sort of sash, do you think?'

But these were entirely women's concerns, and Tom Reid realized that he had no part or parcel in them.

He was quite pleased, therefore, when Mrs Mason called to him from the kitchen and asked him to go down to old Albert Wilde's cottage.

Albert sometimes brought what he called his 'nuncheon' with him ; sometimes he went back home for it. But whichever he did, it was the rarest thing in the world not to see him walking out to the garden to begin work again as Dallicombe church clock started to strike two.

Now, Mrs Mason had suddenly realized that it was nearly half-past two and there was no Albert Wilde down in the vegetable garden lifting her celery for her. Hence her call to Tom for help.

Tom had been long enough with the Masons by now to know where the old gardener lived. His cottage was on the country side of the Doctor's house, that is, the side away from the small town of Dallicombe, and it stood in Manor Lane, running on one side of the Common.

When Tom got there, he found a lorry belonging to the Dallicombe Rural District Council drawn up outside the cottage, blocking the lane, and Albert Wilde standing there arguing with the driver.

The cottage door was open, and from the dark recesses of the interior, Mrs Wilde, whom Tom had never seen before, was watching what took place. She was old and bent and wrinkled, just as Albert was himself, and she had the shrewd, sharp eyes of a peasant ; eyes with which she now watched her man standing up for his rights.

Albert noted Tom's approach and greeted him with the salutation which he invariably used, morning, noon, or night.

' Mus' Tom.'

' Hallo, Mr Wilde.'

' Mrs Mason a-worrying about me up at Long Acre ? '

' Well, she was wondering if you were all right, Mr Wilde.'

' *I'm* all right. 'Tis this lot that's all wrong.'

' This lot ', as a contemptuous jerk of a grimed and horny thumb indicated, meant the D.R.D.C.'s three-ton, rear-and-side-tipping lorry, now deep laden with brick rubble, and its puzzled and rather angry driver.

' No good a-going on at *me*,' he said. ' All I know is I was told to come and tip the stuff here, on the Common.'

' On the Common ? ' Albert replied. ' You ought to know better.'

' Well, that was my orders.'

' 'Oo give 'em you ? '

' The Council, of course. The R.D.C.'

' Ah, the R.D.C. ! ' It did not appear from Albert Wilde's voice that he thought much of the R.D.C. ' There's things a sight older than the R.D.C.,' he went on, ' and the Common's one of 'em.'

' Don't know nothing about that,' the driver said grudgingly.

' Course you don't. *I* don't know nawthing 'bout stron-ermy, but that don't sinnify as all the stars and the stuff about them ain't real, do it ? Do, the Stronemer Royal 'ud look pretty tidy silly, I reckon.'

' All I know is, I've got to tip the stuff on the Common, at least twenty feet clear of the roadside—so the chap in the surveyor's office told me.'

' The chap in the surveyor's office ! I'll wager he doesn't know nothing about Common Land neither. Clurks ! How much stuff are they a-telling you to bring here ? '

'It's from where they're pulling down those old houses in Mill Street. There's a pile of it as big as St Paul's. There'll be fifty or sixty tons, time we finish, I wouldn't wonder.'

'Time *we* finish, you mean,' Albert told him warningly. 'Fast as ever you dump that 'ere stuff on our Common by day, we shall shift it off again by night. *That* I can promise you.'

The driver looked at him uncertainly, and tried to laugh it off.

'You will?' he asked.

'You dump your three tons here by five o'clock this arternoon, and time five o'clock tomorrow morning comes it will all be out in the middle of the highway for the surveyor to play about with.'

The driver gave his unconvincing laugh again.

'In that case,' he said, 'I reckon as I'd better go back to the Council offices and see what they say there.'

'Reckon you had,' Albert Wilde told him severely, 'and let 'em know as there are one or two things left in old England still as they can't mess about with—not if they don't want to stir up a wopses' nest of trouble.'

The discomfited R.D.C. lorry reversed into the main road, and with an unmelodious grinding of gears made off to Dallicombe.

'Proper town chap,' Albert pronounced in strong disapproval, watching the lorry disappear into the distance. 'A furriner.'

He pointed to the acre and a half of open, unfenced, rough grassland that lay on the other side of the lane from his tiny cottage.

'He wanted to dump it *there*,' he said. 'In the middle of the Common. That's what he wanted to do.'

Tom looked out over the Common. It didn't seem very impressive to him; but evidently old Albert Wilde was quite worked up about it.

'And you didn't want him to?' he asked.

'What, on the Common?' Albert asked in a shocked voice. 'There's Common Rights on that land, Mus' Tom. That is, for any one as has got a common holding, same as my bit of a cottage is. Always have been Common Rights as long as old England was. And always will be—provided we look arter them.'

He gave a sly chuckle and went on:

''Course, there *is* a bit o' waste land at the bend of the lane as don't belong to anybody. 'Tis neither Common nor nawthing else. 'E could 'ave tipped his load of nonsense there and no 'arm done. But I weren't a-gooing to tell him that; let him find out for himself. Mrs Mason been a-fidgeting about me, 'as she?'

'She did say something about some celery, Mr Wilde.'

'Love us all! The celery! She wanted it sharp at two o'clock, as well! You coming back up, Mus' Tom?'

Having come thus far away from the Doctor's house, Tom felt disposed to wander about a bit more.

'Well, I don't know,' he said. 'There isn't much to do at the house this afternoon.'

'Plenty for me. I'm all back of my time with this nonsense keeping me here. Why don't you take a walk along the lane and see where the old manor house was?'

'Is there an old manor house along here?'

'Not now there isn't. But there used to be. Manor Lane it's called, and Manor Lane it always was, a-leading up to the old house. The Manor. It stood there time out of mind. But it's gone now.'

'Isn't there anything left to look at?' Tom asked.

'Not a brick above ground now. Only a lot of 'umps and 'ollers. And then, if you swing round left-handed and come up through the beech spinney, you'll find yourself at the bottom of the Doctor's place again.'

So old Albert Wilde turned and stumped off in his slow, steady gait up the road, the short way back to his already neglected work ; and Tom went exploring down Manor Lane.

About half a mile beyond the Wildes' cottage it came to an end. There was a field gate leading into a large arable field, and by the side of the gate a stile. After a moment's hesitation, Tom climbed over the stile and made his way along the headland towards a coppice of beech-trees that bounded the field on the far left-hand side. It was only a ragged little coppice with a small grazing meadow beyond, where five Shorthorn cows looked up in patient surprise at Tom as he walked through them, disturbing their grazing and contemplation. Beyond them was a much bigger beech wood, where the smooth shiny boles went straight up ; clean sticks of timber as sweet as ever a woodman saw anywhere ; and underneath, the ground was brown with the fallen beech leaves not only of last autumn, but of all the autumns since the trees first stood there.

It wasn't too easy to keep a sense of direction in the wood ; but when he finally got to the far edge of it, Tom found that he hadn't done too badly.

There in the dip was the field he already knew quite well, Street Meadow ; and beyond it, where the land rose again gently, the noble remains of a venerable oak-tree in the bottom of Doctor Mason's garden.

Street Meadow. . . .

Tom's eyes were taken off the field for a moment by a movement above him. Something grey, furry, and very alert was watching him from a bough of one of the beech-trees.

A grey squirrel. One of the most difficult things to catch, shoot, or otherwise get rid of in the English countryside. For a moment it stayed quite still, watching its principle enemy, man, and wondering whether this particular example threatened danger or not.

Tom stared back at the cunning little tree-rat, standing for an instant as still as it was itself.

Then very slowly the squirrel began to move. It had made up its mind that he was not dangerous yet but might become so ; and in a leisurely way it was putting the tree trunk between itself and him.

Tom watched it, amused ; and as it began to disappear round the bole of the beech-tree, something a bit odd happened to his eyes.

Suddenly it was as though he were looking through a car windscreen when it's pouring with rain and the wipers aren't working. Everything began to shimmer a bit and to lose its outline. . . .

.   .   .   .   .

It was bright with sunshine, Midsummer Day sunshine. The grass of the field was long and green and was shimmering a little in the heat.

The boy was walking across it with two companions, all three making their way to a group already assembled by the side of the stream. There was a table and a bench. The boy recognized them both as he drew near. They came out of the great hall at the Manor House. Solid, serviceable, oaken stuff made by William the woodwright—well, no, not by him, of course, the boy realized, but perhaps by his grandfather, who had been wood- and wain-wright to the Manor before him, way back in the days of the legendary Dunstan, probably.

Not that the boy bothered about past history much. The past was the past, dead and musty stuff, always cropping up in the garrulous talk of old men. He belonged to the present ; and the present to him. He was seventeen years old and it was Midsummer Day.

The two men walking with him were older than he was. Robert, the one people frequently called Robert the hunter, because he would sooner spend a week in the woods chasing the deer than a day in the big common arable field working, was only about twenty-two ; but the other, Jack, was about forty. He wasn't sure of his own age to a year or so either way. He had an eke-name too. He was known throughout the Hundred as Jack Wildman, and in his youthful heyday there hadn't been a wilder, madder spirit in the place.

As it was Midsummer's Day, the Court Baron of the Manor and the View of Frankpledge should have been held up at the Manor House. Use and custom as far back as man could remember had it so in those parts. By rights, most of the village should have been up at the Manor House, or going to it or coming away ; and not much work would have been done anywhere.

But on this particular Midsummer's Day the age-old custom had for once been broken, and it had been cried throughout the Hundred that the Court Baron and the View of Frankpledge would be held, not on the feast of St John, but in three weeks' time, on the eve of the feast of Saint Swithin.

On this particular Midsummer's Day something unique and extraordinary was on foot ; and most of the village had turned out to see it ; a few of them because they had been warned that they would be wanted, but most of them out of curiosity—curiosity which had a good deal of latent hostility in it.

The boy and the two others with him had been talking about it as they walked towards Street Meadow.

' A book ? ' the boy asked a little uncertainly. The only book which he had seen in his seventeen years was the one from which the priest read when he said Mass each Sunday and feast day.

Jack Wildman laughed. He had travelled farther afield than most in the village, and was never backward in saying so. He had been to Winchester when the great church was building there, and had once by chance poked his head into the stone library where there were more than a score of books.

'Books !' he said contemptuously. 'I've seen 'em in Winchester. Chained to the shelves in case any mortal man should be fool enough to want to make off with 'em. And clurks sitting there bent double, writing all day.'

The boy understood a connection between books and churches ; but here, out in the open in Street Meadow, on a burning hot Midsummer's Day. . . .

'But *this* book,' he persisted. 'This is different, isn't it ?'

'God's oath, it's different,' Robert the hunter answered with his noisy laugh, 'this is some of Norman William's doing, and everything he does is different. This is a book of all England.'

'Of all England ?'

'Of it all. All the shires right up to St Cuthbert's land in the far north, where the great wall is.'

'But what will they write in the book ?' the boy persisted, still puzzled.

'Write ? The names of the manors and of everyone in them, and how much everyone has got, whether of land or beasts or money of any kind, I guess.'

'What for, though ?'

'What for ? What for ? What does anybody ever want to know anything for ? What does the lord of the manor have his court roll of copyhold tenants for ? For work or money, of course. To assess us to see how much we can pay or do. William the Norman wants money. And we've got to pay him. He's got us *here*—like this.'

Robert made a gesture with one of his powerful thumbs.

Jack Wildman laughed. 'Ay,' he said. 'Bottom sawyer gets the dust in his eyes. Must do. 'Tis only nature. But that Norman devil has done some wonderful building. Since

Hastings was fought I've seen some stonework put up in England I shouldn't never have reckoned possible.'

Robert made a face. His own father had fought at Hastings ; his uncle had been killed there.

'We should never have lost at Hastings,' he said, 'and my father often says we wouldn't have done if the axe-men had stood fast, and not run after the Norman horse when they broke.'

'Ah, if, if !' Jack Wildman cried impatiently.

> 'If " ifs " and " ands "
> Were pots and pans
> What would the tinkers do ?

'And if we hadn't lost, what then ? Where should we be ? What good was Harold, anyway ?'

'Good enough to get from Stamford Bridge to Hastings in a fortnight. My father went with him all the way.'

Jack grinned. 'I'm not sorry I missed that bit of hurry-ing,' he said. 'I like to travel ; but it must be in my own time. But, seriously though, Harold was William the Norman's liege-man. He made himself so the year before Hastings, when he was taken prisoner in Normandy. He was a bound man.'

'Well, bound or not, he got a Norman arrow through his eye at Hastings. My father stood close to him on the hill, and heard him cry out. Whatever else that did to him, I reckon it let him out of his bondage anyway. You sound as though you're half-Norman already, Jack Wildman.'

'Me ? I'm half nothing, Robert.' Jack Wildman stopped suddenly and dug his heel into a freshly thrown up mole-hill in Street Meadow, so that the soft earth, warm with mid-summer sun, spilt over his almost bare foot. 'I belong to *this*. The land. There can be all the coming and going you like at the top, but they've all got to come down to this in the end. The Normans can ask what questions they want. I'll tell 'em what I've a mind to, no more.'

' And nothing said touching a certain something we both saw this morning ? ' Robert asked, dropping his voice.

' What don't speak can't lie,' Jack Wildman answered, quoting a favourite saying of one of the old men in the village.

They both laughed ; and the boy, listening, wondered what they were talking about. Something a bit mysterious had crept into the conversation, and he did not know what it was.

Nor was there any time to speculate about it further. They had come near enough to the little group by the stream side to be able to distinguish features and to see who was there, and the boy's interest was caught up in what was going forward.

The massive oak table and the three chairs from the Manor House had been set out not far from the side of the stream, on the flat piece of ground which, according to the old men's stories, had once been a road.

What the old men said was that when they were young the old men of their day had told them that the old men of *their* day had told them—and so it went back, stretching into the dark beginnings of things, making the Past the Present.

' What did the old men of your young days tell you ? ' the boy had once asked.

' About the road. Times gone by there was a road in Street Meadow ; all the way down the valley by the side of the stream. The Romans made it.'

' The Romans ? ' The boy had heard the name, but it meant little to him. ' How long ago ? '

' How long ? ' the old man laughed at the question. ' Who knows ? Before the Confessor ; before Dunstan ; before the Danes ; before all the darkness—a thousand years, maybe.'

And at that the boy had laughed aloud. A thousand

97

years ! What nonsense to talk about a thousand years ago ! He very much doubted if the world itself was as old as that. And at the moment he couldn't care less one way or the other. It was being alive here and now that he cared about ; feeling the sun on his face and bare legs, seeing it light up the colours of the little group they were approaching ; marvelling in his limbs and veins at the very miracle of living.

But all the same, as he walked along that remarkably level stretch of the meadow, he wondered idly if what legend said was true, and that under the turf, if you dug deep enough you would find the stones and the road men talked about ?

' That's William's man sitting at the table,' Jack Wildman said, dropping his voice a little as they came near. ' Proper foxy Norman he looks, too.'

The boy laughed. You had to laugh at the way Jack went on. There was never anything dull about Jack.

And he was right, too, about Hubert de Burgh, which was the name of the man sitting at the oak table, with his long Norman legs in their blue chausses stretched out under it.

De Burgh had sandy hair cut very short, a reddish complexion, and a sharp, turned-up nose which did, undoubtedly, make you think of a fox. Small eyes, he had, close-set and very twinkling and sharp.

The boy was fascinated by him. Although it was twenty years since Hastings had been fought, he himself had set eyes on a Norman of any sort on only half a dozen occasions, and never until this moment on one of quality.

De Burgh had come to England as one of six close friends of the great William : Hubert de Burgh, Hugo de Grant-Mesuil, Walter Giffard, Robert of Solance, William of Coutances, and Roger Mortmain. These were the men William of Normandy had chosen as his friends ; and no man ever chose his friends more carefully. These were among the chief lieutenants who had been with him on that

Michaelmas Day now twenty long years gone by when, at first light, the leading ships of his invading fleet grinded on the pebbles of Pevensey Beach.

They had all been given land a long time since. Well, not all, for two of them fell on the field at Hastings : Roger Mortmain and Robert of Solance. Whenever he thought back to that bloody and tiring day, de Burgh himself always marvelled that it had gone the way it did. Lucky William ! All the great man's friends had always called him that. Maybe, de Burgh thought, you never get to the top in anything without a good slice of luck.

Now, de Burgh did not even know if his old companions were still alive. He did not want to travel, and had been happy and content to settle on his land at Nordfulc, and gradually learn there how to fit in his farming ways with those of the pigheaded Saxons. Pigheaded, and a bit muddle-headed, too, about some things ; but on the whole he was beginning to like them. He was beginning to learn how to get on with them now, and he only hoped his son Rufus would learn too.

He had not wanted to leave his lands in Nordfulc ; but William, who was getting to be an old man now, had sent for him one October day three years ago, and he had had to travel all the way to Westminster, where the big Abbey, which Edward the Confessor had started, was being enlarged and developed.

In Westminster, sitting in that cold, draughty little stone room which he seemed to prefer to all others, William had told him his plan.

It was impossible not to be impressed by William every time you saw him ; and Hubert de Burgh found himself falling again under the old spell. William the Bastard of Falaise ; hard as iron in his body ; quick as lightning in his mind ; true as a blood-brother to his word—a born leader,

99

such as comes into the world of mediocrities every now and again, but none too often.

William always wanted the best in his kingdom ; if any lesser thing got in his way to hinder him, he was capable of getting rid of it quite ruthlessly. This de Burgh knew, as did anyone who had any dealings with the Duke ; and in his respect and affection for the man there was always mingled a little fear.

It had been the last day of October when Hubert reached Westminster and saw the great bulk of the Abbey Church standing in the cornfields by the wide and marshy river. There was a bitterly cold wind blowing, and he wished himself at home in Nordfulc.

When he was shown in to see William in the little dark room, almost the first thing he said was :

' I wonder why you have summoned me to come here and see you ? I'm getting too old for fighting, William.'

' No man is too old for fighting,' the Duke growled. ' Not till he's dead. Or if he is, then he's not properly a man. But fighting ? Who talks of fighting ? '

' You have been known to,' de Burgh suggested, smiling.

' Ay, ay, ay. It will stick to me all my life, that label. And like enough after I'm dead—if men remember anything at all of me, which I doubt. I fight, Hubert de Burgh, when I have to, never else ; and I'd trouble you to remember it.'

' Have I been five days on the road to learn that ? '

' Ay, you have ; and something else. How were the roads, by the way ? '

' Dreadful. Horse-killing, if a man had to push his mount.'

' We must do something about them some day. There haven't been any decent roads made since the Roman days ; but meanwhile, shall I tell you why I sent for you ? '

' I'll not pretend I'm not anxious—for you wouldn't get me here for nothing. That I am certain of.'

Duke William shouted, and his personal servant, the faithful Bolden, who had jumped almost on his heels at the Pevensey landing and had served him ever since, came in.

'Light,' William shouted at him. (Bolden was growing deaf.) 'It's as dark in here as my father's cellar used to be in the castle in Falaise.'

'There are lighter rooms you could use,' Bolden mumbled testily.

'There are ; but I don't choose to,' William answered, laughing indulgently at the other's waywardness. 'I'm a bit set in my ways, Bolden, haven't you noticed that ? '

'As set as a Saxon,' Bolden said, getting the rushlight out from a cupboard let into the stone wall, and working his flint with practised hand.

'And that's saying something,' William ruminated, watching the first ineffectual sparks being struck. 'By all the saints of Normandy, the trouble we've had with the obstinate beggars, eh, Hubert ? When they start talking about Use and Wont, eh ? '

De Burgh had to laugh at that. In the course of some seventeen years he had heard those two words Use and Wont so often that they had become almost like the extra saints' names in the calendar. Saxon right and custom. Saints Use and Wont.

'Saints Use and Wont,' he said aloud.

'Ay, that's about it. I reckon a good Saxon would give up everything else in Mother Church before those two. And when they start talking about " as things were in King Edward's time ", you've either got to hang 'em or agree with 'em, for budge 'em you will *not*.'

De Burgh nodded. He knew the phrase well. It was constantly being used by the middle-aged men, frequently even by the young ; 'as things were in the days of King Edward '.

'You knew the Confessor, didn't you ? ' he asked.

'Of course I knew him,' William snapped, in one of his sudden sharpnesses. 'He was my cousin. Well, not a first cousin, but a near one.'

'So he was.'

'And a holy man—which you and I have never been, Hubert.'

'Well, not specially, I'm afraid.'

'He was the best king this country ever had.'

'Until you came, William.'

'Has coming up to Westminster turned you courtier then, Hubert?'

'Not courtier, William. Just curious.'

'Ay—I've a plan, then. Set that rushlight down now that it's alight, Bolden. There, so ; so that it lights the wall.'

It had been too dark before to see anything of the end wall, but now by the yellow, smoky rushlight, de Burgh saw that a large map hung on it all but covering it, like a work of tapestry.

He had only once before in his life seen a map of any sort ; and never one of this size. He let out an involuntary call of surprise, and William was as delighted as any schoolboy.

'Ah,' he said, 'that *is* a map, isn't it? An old monk in the Abbey here drew it for me, making it large from a little one they have in a book there. *And* putting in a good few places that I've been to and that he knew nothing about.'

De Burgh got up and moved a few paces forward, the better to study this marvel.

'That is what England looks like, then,' he said softly.

'More or less,' William agreed. 'Not that I trust maps too much myself. How can a man make a picture of a whole country? No one has the trick of it. No one is clever enough. But never mind that. This is something.'

'Ay, indeed it is.'

The great Duke rose and put his hand on the map.

'De Burgh,' he said, 'I love this land ; it's more to me now than my own Normandy.'

The other nodded ; he had heard men say, half in jest, half in earnest : 'Duke William has fallen in love with England ; she has bewitched him.'

'I want to make something of it. Something great.'

'You've started already,' de Burgh said, thinking of the great Tower then building in London itself, which he had seen ; of the long Abbey Church at St Albans, which he had heard about ; and of the vast foundations being dug at Ely when he went through the town a year back.

'Ay, we have masons, we can build,' William agreed, guessing what he was referring to, 'but I want knowledge. I want to know.'

'To know ?'

'I want to know about all England—the manors ; who holds them ; of what size they are ; the number of the different sorts of tenants ; the mills ; the markets ; how much land there is. Everything.'

'Of all England !' de Burgh repeated, startled.

'Ay. Of it all. Top to bottom, side to side. Not one manor left out. I want it all set down in a book, to last for ever. Till Doomsday itself come. And you, Hubert, you were always the best of my six at headwork and books ; you've got to help me——'

It was that interview, three years ago, in the cold, dark little room in Westminster, which had brought de Burgh where he was now on Midsummer Day, seated in Street Meadow ready to find out and set down the details of yet one more manor.

Four other principal men had been appointed to help him with the tremendous task, and under them a score of assistants and three dozen copying clerks. It had been methodical work and slow, because William wanted it correct and had impressed

104

that fact on them in no uncertain fashion at the start. But it had been intensely interesting. True, de Burgh was hardly ever in Nordfulc now ; his Saxon bailiff, Howard, had to manage the farm without him ; but he had seen a vast deal of England these last three years, seen it under a microscope ; and he had fallen more in love with it than ever.

Delcum was not a big manor and he had not his full travelling staff with him. Only one of his clerks, Walter, and two men-at-arms. And, of course, Rufus, his son, who had come, not to do any work, but for the fun of the thing.

The men-at-arms were old retainers. One had actually been wounded in the Pevensey fight and bore the marks of it in one withered forearm still ; and the other had served de Burgh almost as long. He brought them with him on this task only nominally as fighting men, for, particularly in the south and the west, he did not expect to find any difficulty or opposition ; in reality they acted as his servants and general helpers.

They were standing behind him now, their leather hauberks old and stained and faded, and their helmets pushed back off their heads, which they still would crop in the old Normandy fashion. They were hot and tired and bored. By his side, on the second of the two stout Saxon chairs which he had borrowed from the Manor House : ' the Duke has need of these '—it was an easy form of borrowing, for no owner was likely to object to lending to the Duke—by his side sat Walter, his faithful clerk.

Walter had gone to school in the huge monastery at Caen, where he had acquired three things : the tonsure, although he gave up training for the priesthood after getting the Minor Orders ; an inordinate liking for wine, which in England he had generally to assuage with mead or ale ; and an uncommon facility in writing.

He was fat ; and on this hot summer day sweat glistened

on his short bare legs, stuck out under the table at which he sat, and ran down on to his dusty worn sandals. A square leather bottle stood on the table; in this he carried his ink, and even at this moment he was dipping his long white quill pen into it.

All these details the boy noticed as he and the two men with him added themselves to the fringe of the little group of people.

The foxy-faced de Burgh; the fat and paper-busy clerk; the bored men-at-arms; the boy saw these and savoured the sharpness of their different temperaments, and thought how good it was to be man alive in a world of such infinite variety.

A goodish lot of the village were there too, he noticed, running his amused, appreciative eye round. Aelrig, the priest; *he* must be in everything, of course. The Lord of the Manor was not there, but Alfred Woodman, his bailiff, was. The bailiff was as you expected a bailiff to be, on the side of the lord and not on the side of the people, but he was not intolerably so. The praepositus of the Manor was there, too: Wilfred, who was one of the villani, owning his own virgate of land in the strips of the common field, and chosen for his post because he was the best husbandman of them all. He could be relied on to see fair play, all right.

Questioning had been going on already for two long hours, and de Burgh had got most of what he wanted. He had learnt by now that he never got quite all the facts. The Saxon devils always hid something; but one way and another, by cracking a joke with them now and again and guessing at what they meant by the things they half-said, he had found out how to get a pretty satisfactory result.

He leant back and clasped his hands behind his head.

'Read out then, Walter, what we have got down so far.'

Walter the clerk cleared his throat, thought for a moment

longingly of what he could do to a full measure of good ale, and started off in a squeaky voice which made everybody smile.

'In the villa where is situated the church of Saint Mary the Virgin in Dalcum, the Lord of the Manor of the same place holds ten and a half hides. There is land for nine plough teams——' There was a slight murmur of protest at this. De Burgh noticed it but said nothing, and the clerk droned on: 'To the demesne belongs seven hides and one virgate, and there are three plough-teams.

'The villeins have five plough-teams; one more might be made; and the villeins hold their land in this wise:

'there is one villanus with one hide; there are eight villani with one virgate each; there are two villani with half a virgate each; there is one cottier with three acres . . .'

Even now, after doing the job for so long, de Burgh still had to translate in his head these outlandish terms, virgate and hide, into something more rational. He always had to make the necessary mental effort to remind himself that what the Saxons called a 'hide' was really 120 acres, and that in every hide there were four virgates. So it looked as though they were returning a total figure of about 1,300 acres for the Manor. He had already ridden round it a couple of times for a quick preliminary glance and to his now expert eye the figure seemed about right. He was getting all this sorted out in his head whilst Walter, needing his ale more than ever, was going on:

'There are twenty-six cottiers paying one shilling each yearly for their gardens. There is meadow for nine plough-teams.'

'That there isn't,' Jack Wildman interjected loudly and

clearly, startling the clerk somewhat and raising a general laugh.

'And wood for fifty pigs,' Walter went on. 'All this as in the time of King Edward.'

'How's that?' de Burgh asked as the clerk ended, tilting his chair back and looking at them.

There was some general talking and discussion as people ran over what they themselves could remember of the facts; but since the information had all been given by the bailiff and the praepositum, who both knew it all intimately in a day-by-day manner, there could hardly be much else except a sort of grudging agreement.

Except over the question of the possibility of carrying another plough-team. Time out of mind since men could remember Dalcum Manor had carried eight plough-teams. Eight plough-teams meant sixty-four working oxen; and there wasn't a man-jack there who was going to be persuaded that the land would support a single beast more.

They said so now, shaking their heads and quoting old saws and harking back to King Edward's day.

De Burgh listened and didn't argue.

'Put eight instead of nine,' he told the clerk suddenly, 'and strike out the part about "one more might be made".'

A murmur of approval went round.

'And the cott garden rents never ought to be a shilling,' a small, thin woman shrilled out indignantly.

'But they are a shilling,' de Burgh replied. 'I'm only writing down what the rents are, not what you would like them to be. What do you want then, Mother? To pay a penny a year and somebody do the digging for you?'

As everybody knew that this was precisely what goodwife Alma did want, there was a laugh of appreciation.

Whilst this had been going on, somebody else had joined

the scene. The boy watched him come up. A young man, eighteen perhaps, or a year more, in a green tunic that looked as fresh and lively as he did himself. A smiling face, and eyes that looked as though they found the whole world a joke to be enjoyed and an everlasting adventure to be explored.

De Burgh saw him come up, too. This was Rufus, the only son left to him. His other boy, Franklin, had been thrown from a horse when he was fifteen and killed at once; and he had two daughters keeping house back in Nordfulc for him. Rufus was the apple of his eye. Wild as a hawk at present; but perhaps that wasn't a bad thing in a youth of eighteen; and maybe before long he would become more serious and take up this painfully slow, but oh, so rewarding, business of making Saxon and Norman one. . . .

Rufus sauntered up and stood close to where the three companions were. The boy, looking at him in frank admiration, caught his eye, and they smiled instinctively at each other.

'Mills?' de Burgh asked. The Duke set great store by mills, water or wind.

Robert the hunter dug Jack unmercifully hard in the ribs, because for the last three years Jack, sobering up a little from his roaming habits, had taken charge of the Manor Mill which clacked away half a mile downstream.

'Yes, there's a mill,' the praepositor answered.

'But it isn't working properly,' Jack called out.

'Not working?' de Burgh asked. 'Why?'

'Stones want re-dressing,' Jack replied with the instant readiness of the accomplished liar. 'And anyway, the teeth in the crown wheel are all worn away.'

Robert, listening to his companion, laughed. He knew just how much truth there was in what Jack said—and that wasn't a great deal—and he knew just why Jack said it: partly out of a constitutional dislike of giving any foreigner any information at all, and partly in a vague hope that what-

109

ever tax was ultimately going to be levied on the mill might be lessened by his poor account of it.

'It was working all right this morning when I was there.'

The high, clear, cheerful voice of young Rufus de Burgh startled every one.

'And when was that?' Jack Wildman inquired sourly.

'This morning. Early. I was trying to catch a trout in the pool below the tail-race.'

Instantly there was a general murmur of disapproval. Time out of mind the right of fishing in the stream between what was called Roman Post and the glebe land had belonged to the commoners of the Manor.

De Burgh didn't know this in detail, but he guessed that something of the sort must be so from the reaction of the Saxons standing round. And if he hadn't been on the Duke's business he could have laughed aloud. These Saxons! Poachers to a man, all of them. They'd steal the pheasant from your very pot. But you take half a pinch of fur or feather from any living thing in territory they considered their own by ancient right, and you might as well sit down bare-breeched in a hornets' nest.

Least said soonest mended about the trout in the tail-race pool, he thought, so he tilted his chair back again, stared over the heads of the still virtuously indignant Saxons and said:

'Any treasure trove found in the last year within the Manor?'

It was a silly question, and he knew it was. He only asked it to divert attention, and because the Duke insisted on it. William of Falaise was a great man, no question, but, like every other mortal man de Burgh had ever known, he dearly loved the chink of gold. Maybe he needed it, for hammering England into shape after all the torn-about time she'd been through was an expensive business. At any rate, he had laid it down flat and final: all treasure trove belonged to the Crown ; anybody's findings was the King's keepings.

So the question had to be asked ; and it was answered, as de Burgh expected, by silence. But the boy was aware of a quick glance between his two companions.

'Touching the glebe—' de Burgh continued ; and just then, out of the corner of his eye, the boy saw a movement. Young Rufus de Burgh had brought the short bow he carried round to his hand and was slowly raising it into position, fitting an arrow into place as he did so.

He had spotted a coney that was sitting sunning itself on the far side of the stream. Jack Wildman had seen it too ; and just as young de Burgh hauled the bowstring back to the lobe of his right ear, Jack, for devilment, clapped his hands together loudly.

The coney, startled by the noise, instantly began to lope away, and instead of hitting it fair and square and scoring an immediate kill, young de Burgh's amazingly accurate arrow pierced one hind leg, splintering the bone.

The animal was half-stunned by the shock and lost its sense of direction. Uncertainly and lop-sided, it began to go flip-flop, flip-flop, away from its burrow.

Without a second's hesitation Rufus de Burgh flung his bow away and ran after his quarry.

'Sport, sport !' Jack Wildman cried. 'Don't let 'un get it, boy, don't let 'un get it. *Run.*'

Jack couldn't run much himself because of the fall he had taken from the tower of Dalcum church years before. Everybody knew that. The boy knew it, and remembered it, in the same instant that Jack's hand clapped him on the shoulder and Jack's laughing, urgent voice called out : 'Run, run !'

And the boy *could* run. Every May-day when the games were held he outran them all. So now, although the young Norman had a lead, the boy started after him like the wind, the excitement and the fun of the thing giving him wings.

'Whau, whoop!' screamed Jack encouragingly, 'leu, leu, leu, *whooooop!*'

Others shouted with him and everybody laughed; and de Burgh, wise old Hubert de Burgh, laughed with them. It interrupted business, of course; but it made for friendship.

'By the Mass, how that Saxon boy can run,' he thought.

The boy was going flat out. Vague thoughts were chasing through his head that this was a Saxon versus Norman affair, and that it would be gratifying to beat the Norman; but mostly he was running just for the fun of it.

'St Christopher, he'll get there first yet,' Jack cried in admiration, putting his left hand up to his ear and letting out another piercing hunting-cry: '*Whau, whooooop!*'

'Got the measure of him,' the boy thought, noting the distance yet to go to the limping rabbit, and how the space between himself and young de Burgh was steadily decreasing.

'One more burst——'

That's a lovely feeling in any race or game, when your measuring eye assures you that you needn't worry; keep going and the thing is yours. A lovely feeling; but the boy had no time to enjoy it, for the thought had hardly come into his head before it, and all else, too, for the moment, was knocked clean out of him.

He was actually on the Norman's heels when—*crash!* He caught his foot in a tangle of brambles hidden in a tussock of grass, and came down a most almighty purler flat on his face, knocking half the senses and all the wind out of himself.

It was five long seconds before he was really aware of anything; then for five more all he could think about was the stabbing agony of trying to take breath.

'Gur-ur-ur,' he gasped painfully.

'Easy,' laughed Rufus de Burgh sympathetically, 'easy. It'll come.'

'Ur, ur.' The boy gave a great gasp like a landed fish and felt suddenly easier. 'That's better,' he said.

Rufus was standing over him, with a friendly hand on his shoulder.

'You didn't go after the coney?' the Saxon boy asked, wondering a little.

'I heard you fall just behind me so I turned to see if you were hurt.'

'Oh—not hurt; only the breathing knocked out of me.'

'You must have good legs,' Rufus said in admiration, 'for I had a start and I can run fast. Up.'

He held out his hand and the boy, grasping it, came easily to his feet, himself again now.

There was friendship in that grasp; and for an instant the two young men looked smilingly at each other. . . .

When all the questioning was over, and the grumbles and comments and complaints done with, the boy found himself walking back towards the mill with his two companions.

'But what I said was perfectly true,' Jack was answering in reply to Robert, who had been teasing him about the mill, 'the teeth in the crown-wheel *are* all worn; badly.'

'Of course they are. And have been any time these last six years.'

'That's as may be. I said nothing of that. *And* the stones want dressing.'

''Course they do. They want dressing every six months. And you dress 'em every six months because you've got the knack of it, none better.'

'I learnt it from a Frenchman in Gloucester, time I was there with my father. They use a different cut from us with the chisel, and the stones grind more evenly.'

Do-Little Mill was the highest up on the stream; hence

the name some wag had bestowed on it when it was built in the time of King Edward.

It was a two-storied timber building with the upper floor carried on beams generous enough to support an army. The inside was dark and cobwebby and always dusty from the fine powder of ground meal. When the sluice was raised outside and the water came thundering down into the buckets of the overshot wheel the whole building shook with the tumult and vibration of it ; and inside, the crown-wheel with its box-wood teeth went lumberingly, ponderously, creakingly round on its remorseless work.

But now the sluice was shut and the stream was running to waste in a steady miniature waterfall through the vent in the side of the leat.

' Any corn to be ground ? ' the boy asked hopefully.

' There's always corn to be ground,' Jack Wildman answered, adding easily, ' and time to do it in. Can you use a spade, youngster, and keep your mouth shut ? '

The boy laughed. ' As well as most,' he said, wondering what was coming.

' Ever seen the like of these ? ' Wildman asked.

The boy took the three proffered coins and turned them over in his hand, marvelling at their colour.

' Money ? ' he said at last.

' Ay. Gold.'

' *Gold ?* And with writing, too.'

' They put lettering on coins,' Wildman explained airily, ' but what it means only God knows. I don't. I can't read. But never mind the writing. Gold's gold all England over. Always has been, always will be.'

' How came you by them ? '

Wildman smiled at him slyly and made answer.

' One of the priest's angels must have dropped them, I reckon, on the long sling at the back of the mill which I dig

115

for a garden ; and pay a shilling a year for, which old Mother Alma was croaking about.'

' Did he now ? ' the boy replied, wondering what the real explanation was.

' Look,' Wildman went on, changing and dropping his tone, so that instinctively the three of them drew together as conspirators might. ' A cott stood here long before the mill was built. Some old chap living by himself most likely ; an out-of-the-way place it would be then. I reckon that when the dark times came and those devils of Danes came burning and killing and busting everything up, a lot of people must have scraped a hole somewhere in the garden and hidden what bit of money they had away in it for safety. I've heard tell of it before from other parts. The people who lived here may have done it ; and then the Danes came and killed them just the same, and nobody knew anything about it. Till I was digging only yesterday and these came glittering up.'

' Funny how they aren't tarnished,' Robert said, picking up one of the coins again.

' Gold doesn't tarnish. Not real gold. Never. You know what Norman law says : where there's three there's a crowd. What I say is : *where there's three there might be a crowd*. Let's look and see.'

' And Norman law says treasure trove goes to the King,' Robert reminded him.

Jack grinned in his impudent way. ' I'm wonderfully deaf of one ear,' he said, ' and somehow I never heard that bit. Come on.'

Three wooden spades stood against the wall. They each took one, and Jack led the way out of the dark interior of the mill into the bright sunlight of the little strip of garden.

' Get a pick from the shed, Robert,' he ordered, ' and let's see what we can do.'

' But how do you know where to dig ? ' the boy asked.

'I don't know. I'm guessing. Knowledge is a dangerous thing—isn't the priest always telling us that? Well, I don't mind admitting I could do with a bit of danger at this moment; it might save a mortal lot of work.'

The three of them worked for three long hours till the shadows lengthened and the brightness began to fade out of the day. Failure to find anything only made Jack more obstinate than ever.

'I'll dig all night if need be,' he cried.

But he didn't have to, for at that instant Robert's wooden spade scraped against something that certainly wasn't earth, and he sang out : 'Hold hard—what have I got here?'

Wildman was on his knees in an instant, exploring carefully with his hands. Finally he gave a little cry of triumph under his breath.

'Leu, leu, leu,' he chattered as he got to his feet again. 'What about that, eh? Didn't I tell you the angels had been this way dropping things?'

He held up a pot as big as a pig's bladder when it is blown up for the sport of kicking. It was of red earthenware, still with some faint traces of colour on the outside, and quite unbroken.

'They had good workmanship even in those old times,' Robert said admiringly.

'Ay, ay, ay. But we aren't admiring the way they made pots,' Wildman answered testily. 'What's in it? That's what we want to know. It's heavy enough.'

He put the pot on the freshly dug, dark loamy earth and hit it hard with the edge of his wooden spade. The earthenware cracked at once and the pot fell in two. And from the middle of it came out a yellow surging of coins.

The boy and the two men stared at the sight.

'God and His holy saints!' Wildman said softly. 'What did I tell you?'

117

It took him at least five minutes to count them, because counting was not a thing that came easily to him, or to either of the others ; and he could only accomplish it by arranging the coins in separate groups of ten. In the end there were five such groups, with two coins over, and the final tally was twelve gold coins like the three they already had and forty silver ones, which were all greatly discoloured.

The boy had never seen fifty-two coins together at one time in his life before. Nor had either of the others, for money was not a thing which was used much in the village. They were all three standing staring at their exciting find when Robert said quietly :

'Don't turn round or move quickly, but someone is standing at the end of the garden-sling watching us, and I think it is young de Burgh.'

Luckily there was a piece of old brown sacking thrown out of the mill lying close by on the ground ; and without a moment's hesitation, Wildman, whose mind always worked quickly in a crisis, kicked it over the pot and the coins, covering all up.

Then he turned and there was young Rufus de Burgh standing at the far end of the garden-sling and looking over the quick-set hedge, just as Robert had said.

The three of them had been standing between their find and the unwelcome Norman behind them, and it was by no means certain that he had been able to see anything that mattered. The boy realized this ; and he knew that Wildman must be thinking along the same lines by the way he spoke, for Jack's voice was neither hostile nor friendly. He thought it best to feel his way for a bit and find out how things stood.

'Come fishing again ? ' he inquired.

Young de Burgh laughed, and once again the boy found himself smiling instinctively for the freshness and charm in the other's face.

'My father was cross with me over that,' he said. 'I didn't know that all men might not fish in the water.'

Wildman laughed. 'No harm done,' he said. 'I reckon the sun'll rise tomorrow morning just the same in spite of it. Did you catch anything?'

'I saw a big fellow in the shallow pool where the bank hollows out.'

'Ah. I know him. Baldy, I call him. He's been there as long as I've had the mill. As fat as a monk and twice as cunning.'

Rufus de Burgh put one hand on a rail in the hedge and vaulted over easily. He walked down the garden with that pleasant air of assurance which comes from being not yet twenty and fit as a fiddle, and finding the whole wide world a wonderfully exciting place to be in.

The three Saxons watched him coming and said nothing. But the air was tense suddenly. Out of the corner of his eye the boy was aware that Jack Wildman had moved ever so slightly. He was shifting his weight; getting balanced; making ready to spring.

'If de Burgh asks what is under the sacking and makes any attempt to find out, Jack will go for him,' the boy thought. And he didn't want it to happen. Desperately he didn't. Not altogether because of the mortal danger they would then all three be in; but because he felt such a strong liking for happy, carefree young Rufus de Burgh.

Jack Wildman shifted his weight and made ready and watched as a fox watches in the woodland ride; but he did not move. He did not want to have to move. To kill a Norman, to injure one, even to raise your hand against one, meant only one thing—death. True, there was talk all the time of acting together; of one helping the other; of Saxon and Norman being brothers. 'But,' thought Wildman bitterly, 'it stops at talk. If I lay hand on this young gamecock out of Normandy I shall be an outlawed man ; hunted ; and if they catch me I'll have my throat slit quicker than a Christmas pig. That's the way that hard old devil up at Westminster has laid it down, and that's the way it is.

'*But all the same*,' his thoughts ran on, '*I'll do it.* If he so much as makes to touch that bit of sacking I'm going for him. What I dig in my garden I reckon is *mine* and I'm not giving it up for all the swaggering, armour-clad knights that come lumbering from across the sea. . . .'

Rufus de Burgh stopped when he reached the group of three and smiled at them. Maybe he was aware of a tenseness in the atmosphere, but he made no comment on it ; all he said was, speaking in a casual way :

' Your greenstuff looks wonderfully well.' (' Talk to 'em about the weather, about one of the games they play, or about their gardens, and you'll get on,' his father's shrewd advice came back to him and he acted on it.)

At once the atmosphere eased very slightly but perceptibly. Jack Wildman thought a lot of his garden at the Mill. If anyone else in the whole Hundred grew better peas and beans he would like to know who they were.

' Not too bad,' he agreed. ' It's the river soil as makes the stuff come on. The mud.'

' *Now*,' thought the boy, ' *he'll ask what all the digging has been for, and—*'

Perhaps Wildman thought the same thing and had a mind to bring the crisis on, for he said softly :

' But I don't think you walked down to the Mill to look at my garden ? '

Young de Burgh threw his handsome head back and laughed.

' By Saint Cross, no, I didn't,' he cried. ' I'm no gardener. Adam dug, the priests say ; let him dig and welcome, say I, but who did the hunting ? '

'Hunting?' All three Saxon heads were raised sharply at that word.

'I came to see if there was a bit of sport to be had. Look, my father is shut up in the parlour of the Manor House with that fat clerk Walter writing, writing, writing. Domesday Book, Duke William calls his fad. I say it won't be finished till Doomsday, the way they are going on. I've no mind to be inside writing or reading. Every man to his trade. Let clerks do that. I've a mind for a bit of sport, and I had a notion you might find it for me.'

'Fishing?'

Rufus de Burgh looked steadily at Jack Wildman, shook his head slowly, and said at last:

'No, not fishing. Runs there nothing in the woods of this manor?'

That made a silence; a very definite and sharp silence, like thin ice forming fast on the top of shallow water.

The boy felt Robert the hunter stir at his side, as though the very thought of a wild thing running in the wood made him restless. For a moment Jack Wildman said nothing. But he was thinking fast and furious.

Did nothing run in the woods? By all the saints in the calendar, something did run there. The tall red deer, the hunting of which was the Norman King's especial and peculiar delight; and the delight, too, of every man with a drop of real blood in his veins. Only, if he were a Saxon, he must not do it; for the red deer belonged to the King.

What Jack was thinking was that there might be something in this brotherhood business after all, for if they were all caught running deer in the woods and young de Burgh was with them and in the game, things would not be so likely to go hard with them. Moreover, if the young Norman had spotted anything of the treasure trove, he would be hardly likely to say anything about that if they were all partners in another escapade together. And on top of all, he dearly loved a day after the deer, did Jack Wildman.

So did Robert ; even more than the other man, for with Robert, hunting was a passion ; and it was his fat chuckle that now broke the silence.

' I can show you all there is to be seen in the woods,' he said. ' There's sport and to spare if you know where to look for it. But what about those two serving men of your father's ? '

' Within doors. In the Manor House, sitting in the rushes of the Great Hall and drinking ale out of leather bottles as though there was nothing else in the wide world to do. As long as my father is shut away with Walter the Clerk in the parlour writing they'll sit there drinking. No need to worry about them.'

' The bailiff ? '

' The bailiff and the other one—what do you call him ? '

' The praepositus ? '

' Ay. They are both there, closeted with my father, answering questions.'

' What are we waiting for, then ? ' Robert asked with another chuckle. ' A man must have a bit of sport sometimes, eh, Jack ? '

' Or be hanged else,' Wildman answered, laughing with him. He was quite persuaded now ; it would not be the first time, no, nor the fifty-first, that he had done a bit of poaching ; and with all the people who were likely to be a nuisance shut up in the Manor House cudgelling their brains over this great book of Duke William's, there seemed to be no reason why honest men shouldn't enjoy themselves for an hour or so. And to rouse and run a deer with a young Norman to help would be something of a novelty at least.

' What about dogs ? ' he asked, business-like all of a sudden.

' I can bring my Snapper,' Robert said.

122

Wildman nodded. Robert's tall brown hound Snapper was a character in the village, and there wasn't a better dog to work in the woods for five miles round.

'Snapper will do,' he agreed, 'and the four of us. Take the young Norman with you, Robert, to get your dog and anything else you need; and where shall we meet? By the Long Stone?'

Robert shook his head. 'Not so far up the slope,' he counselled, 'the deer haven't harboured in that part of the wood since last back-end. We shall do better to start at the old spring.'

'By the old spring then. The youngster can come with me and we'll meet you two there as soon as you like.'

'Within the half hour.'

'No later. And, Robert——'

'What now?'

'No need to cry anything abroad. The fewer people who see you and the Norman together the better.'

'Anyone will have to be mighty sharp to spot us the way I shall go, never fear,' Robert assured him. 'Come on, Master de Burgh.'

As soon as they were gone, Jack Wildman winked at the boy.

'Did he spot anything, think you?'

'I don't think so. I was standing right between him and the pot of money. Besides, he would surely have said something, wouldn't he?'

'Ay. I think he would. So we find treasure and go hunting deer all in one day, eh? Well, I'd liefer wear out than rust any day, as they say, so what of it? And I've known worse eating than the hindquarters of a buck, by a long way. First, though, I think we'll put this indoors.'

He pulled the sacking away and, gathering up the two halves of the broken pot and all the coins, took them into the mill, the boy following. As many as two dozen sacks full of corn were standing waiting to be dealt with, and Jack stowed his treasure away in the dusty darkness behind them.

'If I left it there for a twelvemonth nobody but rats would know anything about it,' he shouted. (In the mill you had to shout because of the thunder of the water.) Having dealt with that, he prized a loose stone out of one wall and put his arm into the long narrow recess behind it.

He drew out a three-quarter size bow, not the type with the long continuous curve such as the archers used in battle, but the lighter, hunting sort, shaped at the hold for the grip of the left hand.

This, of course, did not surprise the boy in the slightest. Ever since he could remember he was used to the fact that in three Saxon houses out of every four a hunting weapon of some sort, be it bow or knife or spear, was hidden. The Norman law forbade the keeping of any such weapons and, officially, said that the penalty for being found with them was death. But that was up at Westminster (did they hunt up there? the boy wondered), or within the boundaries of Royal Forests such as the great forest of Essemore in the west; in most other places the law was not very rigorously applied.

'What will you hunt with?' Jack Wildman asked. 'I've but the one bow.'

'My feet. I'll run with Snapper.'

'And if you run as fast as you were going after that wounded coney in Street Meadow this afternoon, I reckon Snapper will have his work cut out to keep up with you. I liked to see you beating the Norman.'

'It was good of him to stop and help me when I fell.'

'Ay. He looks a likely enough lad. But — he's a Norman.'

'I like him.'

'You're not twenty and I'm past forty. There's the

124

difference. Come on, boy. If we stay here talking all day the other two will be hunting without us.'

The great wood where they were all to meet clothed the slopes of two hills and the deep combe between them a matter of a mile away from the village. They saw only a couple of people on their way, and to their salutation Jack shouted out a purposely unintelligible reply which might have meant anything, and which certainly gave nothing away.

By this time it was past eight o'clock in the evening, and although it was still full light out in the fields it was a different matter once they actually got into Lady Wood.

' The tall oaks of Lady Wood, there they growed and there they stood.' Jack quoted the old ale-house jingle affectionately as he led the way into the gloomy greenness under the trees. He had said the selfsame words every time he went into the wood in the past, and would doubtless say them on every such occasion in the future. He was a man of set habit in some things, was Jack Wildman.

And also a man of infinite cunning in woodcraft. He hardly abated his pace one jot and there was little enough to guide him by way of track, but he never seemed to be at fault for direction, and he moved with the absolute minimum of noise.

The boy walked behind him, thus lessening the danger of making any sound ; only once before had he been out on a full-scale poaching expedition and his pulses were tingling with excitement. He wouldn't, at that moment, have changed places with any man in the kingdom.

' I would have gone to the Long Stone,' Jack said over his shoulder in a whisper, ' but Robert says the spring, and he has a knack of knowing where the beasts lie up.'

The boy nodded. He would have gone with equal happiness to either trysting place, or to any other, so long as that he was in the fun somehow.

125

There was this much to be said for the spring—it was a good deal nearer ; but even so, twenty minutes had gone by before Jack led them into a bit of a clearing where, by a marshy, boggy spot in the ground, they saw the other two. So quietly had Jack and the boy come on the scene that just for an instant the beginnings of a growl began to rumble in the long yellow dog's throat ; but instantly, and without any finesse or preamble, his master kicked him hard in the ribs.

'*Quiet*,' he whispered savagely ; a dog that growled or barked out hunting was worse than useless.

Snapper subsided and the four poachers greeted one another, Jack Wildman and Robert exchanging a nod, and Rufus de Burgh smiling at the boy.

Robert took command because he knew most about the deer. He was carrying a bow very much like the one Jack had, only shorter and older, the wood shiny with much handling ; and when he spoke it was in a low voice not much above a whisper.

'They've been wont to harbour here this last month or two,' he said. 'If we follow where the water goes we'll see signs of 'em, surely.'

So the four of them—five, if you counted Snapper, close to his master's heels, began to walk in single file along the narrow clearing, spongy with moisture, yet scarcely a proper stream, which led towards the side of the wood called Priest's Part.

Robert went first, then Jack Wildman, both of them with their eyes fixed attentively on the ground ; then came Rufus de Burgh and close behind him the boy.

Rufus threw a quick smile over his shoulder and asked quietly :

'Do you know the marks ?'

'Not all that well,' the boy had to confess. 'Not as well as those two in front.'

'Nor I,' Rufus said, 'but it's fun all the same, isn't it?'
The boy nodded. 'Marvellous.'

Robert went slowly, and every now and again he shook his head in disapproval. No tell-tale slot was visible in the soft ground and it began to seem as though the deer must have given up using that part of the wood.

After the remembered heat of the afternoon out in Street Meadow it was cool in the wood, where the evening air hung motionless beneath the huge green trees and little clouds of midges hung and hummed.

'We'd have done better to go to the Long Stone after all,' Robert said after a while. 'They've changed their habits seemingly.'

'What's begun must be gone on with,' Jack advised; 'we've all night yet.'

So they plodded on, the wood growing denser on either side. Then suddenly there was a clearing; no more than a V cut in the trees as a man cuts a piece of cheese with a knife, and for a moment they could look out over the village.

The two men in front went on, hardly lifting their heads, but both Rufus the Norman and the Saxon boy stopped instinctively.

The boy had never seen that view of his village before. It lay beneath him now; a thing in miniature, like the wonderful little coloured pictures that with sure and steady hands the old monks painted into the first letters of their holy books.

He could see the church of St Mary on its little hill, the glebe land of the priest, the great common field where the corn stood ripening in the strips, and the huge common meadow reaching down towards the stream. There, too, was the Manor House and, mostly in a cluster in the middle, but here and there in twos and singly, the cottages, huts, and hovels, with the blue wood smoke rising straight up into the still evening air from a score of hearths.

The boy had never been conscious of it as a whole, as an entity, before. And now, seeing it thus for the first time, it came into his heart that it was his home and that he loved it.

Rufus, standing close to him, whispered over his shoulder : ' I like your English villages ; they look homely.' And the boy was grateful to him for saying it.

When they caught up the two men and the hound in front it was at a spot where the forest had thinned away and the open ground spread in a rough circle, with the marshy line of the little stream running through the middle of it.

Robert the hunter was on his knees with Jack bending over him ; and they were both looking at the ground intently.

' There he is,' Robert was saying, ' there's His Lordship.'

' Leu, leu, leu,' Jack clucked under his breath, ' that's no lightweight.'

' Biggest slot I've ever seen——'

' And fresh made by the looks of it.'

Robert studied the slot marks long and closely before he gave a verdict. He noted the size of them, the deepness of the impression, their evenness.

' Ay, that's a monster,' he said at last. ' A stag, of course, and in no hurry. Walking only. Full-fed, I should say, and he came here to drink—see where the marks are deeper than the rest because he stood ? Then he turns, you can see it, and goes off to find somewhere to lie up for the night. He'll not walk far—who does after supper and his pot of ale ? And when we find him he'll be worth finding, that I warrant you.'

It was easy enough to follow the big fellow's slot for some twenty or thirty yards, because he had walked along in the boggy part and had left his marks ; but when he turned and took to the summer-hard ground, there was nothing, the boy thought, to show which way they should follow.

But Robert was not in doubt for an instant.

' His Lordship won't want to lie up among the trees,' he

counselled. 'The wood runs into a narrow belt here—the Maiden's Girdle, they call it—and beyond there's a great wide open part with fern and bracken. That's where he'll be.'

He put a forefinger in his mouth, sucked it, and held it up above his head to test the wind.

'If there's any wind at all,' he whispered, 'it's against us, so we needn't worry about that. Gently now, and mind where you tread.'

So now with the sense of expectancy and excitement growing every moment, they went on, Robert in front again and all of them being extra cautious to go quietly.

The tall oaks stood thickly together in the narrow tongue of wood known as the Maiden's Girdle and there was a gloomy greeny darkness between them.

Once young Rufus stumbled over a fallen oak branch hidden in a tangle of undergrowth and made some noise, and Jack growled back at him: 'Curse you, you clumsy young Norman devil. Pick up your feet, can't you?' The boy could see the angry flush that suffused young de Burgh's face. He was not used to being spoken to in that way by anyone, least of all by a Saxon; and for an instant there were hot and angry words on his lips. But he swallowed them and said nothing; and from in front Robert hissed back urgently:

'Steady, steady. Viewed 'un, viewed 'un.'

The four of them stood stock still for what seemed an eternity to the boy; then Robert made a gentle beckoning gesture with his hand, and with infinite caution and quiet the others came up level with him.

Robert had halted on the far side of the narrow neck of wood, and now they were all looking out over a wide open plateau of coarse land largely covered with bracken and fern, beyond which, half a mile away maybe, the dark woods closed round again with an open gap in the centre.

But it was not at the far ring of dark green trees they

were looking, for in the middle distance, clear and unmistakable under the full moon which had already made silver nonsense of the June twilight, lay His Lordship. A great stag.

He had trampled and rolled a comfortable place in the bracken for himself and there he was now, crouched, at ease and indolent, suspecting nothing and supremely well-content.

As they watched in silence, the beast rose easily to shift his position and it was possible to see what a noble animal he was.

'Brow bay and trey and three a-top,' Robert muttered under his breath, reckoning up his points. 'Holy Virgin, what a gurt big old monster.'

The boy felt his heart thudding a little from sheer excitement and he wondered what would happen next ; for if they moved out of the cover of the trees the stag would surely see them and be off ; and there was as yet no question of drawing a bow, for the beast stood three or four full bow-shots away.

They watched in silence while the stag turned thrice in his own length, and as many times put his head to the ground, almost like a dog circling in a bed of straw. At length, satisfied that he had got things as comfortable as possible, he lowered himself down again with an out-blown ' *ugh* '—just like an old man, the boy thought, who sits down gratefully in the fireside corner.

Robert stood there gazing at the sight as though he could never see his fill of it, but presently he turned and made a gesture that they should all go back into the wood.

When they had gone some fifty yards or more and were well hidden once again among the trees, he said in a whisper, his eyes glistening with pure excitement :

' Hunt's up, my lads. He's ours if we go careful.'

' What shall we do ? ' Rufus de Burgh asked impetuously. ' All run out on him together ? '

' Talk sense ! ' Robert told him with withering scorn in his voice. ' All run out on him together ! They must teach you queer hunting in Normandy. If we go that way about it we shall have His Lordship in the next hundred within ten minutes, and we shall see no more than half the backside of him whilst he makes off. What we've to do is to keep him to the woods. Then we shall stand a chance.'

'He mustn't get away across the open,' Jack Wildman put in.

'Of course not. If he does he'll be through Pulpit Gap in the far woods, and we might as well whistle and all go home. Now listen . . .'

So Robert the hunter laid his plan.

It was the old, old story that has run through the world since time began : Man, the slow-moving, short-winded, weak-limbed animal encompassing the death of things faster, stronger, nobler than himself because in his small tight skull there are a few more whorls of grey thinking-matter than in theirs.

'Keep him to the woods where his speed won't avail him so much, and there we can so turn and twist and harry him, sending him this way and that till he's boxed-up and made stupid with fear, that we shall be able to close in on him at last and chop him down . . .'

Such was the essence of Robert's hunting plan ; and to accomplish it Rufus de Burgh and the boy were to make a wide circuit and to work their way round well beyond the stag, between him and the gap in the far arm of wood through which he would naturally try to run into the waste land on the other side. They were not to be together, Robert told them, but a hundred yards apart. He would give them good time to get where he wanted them, and when they heard him hoot like an owl they were to stand up, moving their arms up and down on either side. 'No noise,' he told them, 'just flap like an old hen does.' Then they were to begin to close in slowly and steadily on the stag.

131

If Robert gave his owl's hoot a second time they were to start running.

'Once we get him in the woods,' Robert concluded, 'running to and fro and moithered, we shall stand a chance. Now off you go, you two.'

'Look up at the skyline to know where you are,' was his last whispered counsel, 'and listen for the owl-hoot'; and with these admonitions in their ears, the boy and young Rufus de Burgh began to cast a wide, cautious half-circle to the right which would bring them well the other side of their yet unsuspecting quarry.

The boy kept his eyes up as Robert had told him and in the silver moonlight picked out the top of a particularly tall oak standing well above the general level of the others to serve as a mark. They went in silence and almost bent double, casting wide at first and then beginning to work round again. When the boy judged they had gone far enough he left Rufus behind, bidding him stay still, and himself went on alone for another hundred paces and then knelt in the grass.

Robert was as good as his word about giving them time to get to their places, and the boy was just beginning to wonder if something had miscarried somewhere, so long did the silence seem, when the night air trembled with the solitary, long-drawn out, eerie ' *tuwhit tu-whooooo* ' of an owl's cry.

It was perfectly done ; so perfectly that for a moment the boy questioned whether it was Robert, or a real owl after all ; but he stood up, and he could see that Rufus had done the same.

Then they both began to walk forward steadily, moving their arms up and down on either side in a flapping motion.

The stag instantly became aware of something and lifted his great head to confirm what he thought he had heard. Finding that he was right, he rose reluctantly—for he was full-fed and sleepy—gathering his legs together and arching his back and stretching himself. He turned round slowly, testing the wind, and then stood at gaze for a moment or two watching the two figures approaching him.

He was annoyed at being disturbed but he was not particularly frightened. He had met this enemy Man before and knew something about him. There were not enough of them here to be dangerous, he judged ; nor were they near enough.

He turned and began to walk back towards the main part of the wood, every now and again tossing his great head in indignation at being disturbed.

Robert the hunter and Jack Wildman, watching all this, smiled. This was just as they wanted things to happen. They were well hidden in the trees ; they were down-wind ; and the stag's attention was naturally focussed behind him on the two men who walked in his wake with such silly, yet disturbing movements.

Robert began to estimate the paces and shifted his left hand a little to get a better grip on his bow. He was not well off for arrows—he only had three—and so could not afford to waste one. He reckoned that another twenty yards would bring the stag within bow-shot ; not that he was going to draw on him at that extreme range, of course. Some excitable young fool out on his first night's poaching beneath the shining moon might lose his head and act that way. Robert had long since learnt to steady his thumping heart, to quieten his racing pulse, to ignore the dry tautness that pure excitement could bring suddenly into the throat, and to bide his time.

He did so now ; and it looked as though all must go right.

He swallowed his spittle and with infinite caution began to bring his bow up to the ready.

He had hardly started to do so when the stag suddenly stopped in his tracks and stood at gaze once more.

Robert's left hand froze to his side and silently he called on all the devils he knew to tell him what was the matter.

The stag couldn't have heard him because he had made no noise, and Jack Wildman at his side was standing as still as a statue in holy rood-screen. The wind was blowing towards them and so their scent could not have betrayed them. What then?

What then, indeed? He realized that it was profitless to ask the question, for he would never know the answer.

Something had warned the oncoming stag at a vital moment; and now they would never know what it was. Nor did it matter much, for there His Lordship was, his great antlered head raised in the moonlight, apprehensive and very much on his guard.

Robert wished urgently then that there were three men beyond doing the driving, for if the stag now decided to double back and make for Pulpit Gap nothing could stop him. It was imperative to increase the fear behind him and get him moving again, and Robert wetted his lips quickly, sucked in his cheeks, threw back his head, and once again made the melodiously melancholy cry of an owl.

The move was not without its danger, for although the stag had no idea that the cry did not in fact come from an owl, he might well ask himself, Robert realized, why the owl made the noise. He evidently had some slight, unformed suspicion already of the dark piece of wood in front of him, and anything at all which might give support to that dawning suspicion would be magnified by him and given undue weight.

So it was a risk to give that second owl's cry; but a risk that, on balance, had to be taken.

Rufus de Burgh and the boy, hearing the signal, acted on it immediately. Instead of walking slowly as they had been doing they now began to run.

The boy hadn't gone a dozen yards before he stumbled against some obstruction in the rough bracken and came noisily to his knees. He was up again in an instant, unhurt and all but crying with vexation at having made such a blunder ; but as a matter of fact it was his very stumbling that, for the moment, saved the situation.

The stag, for the first time beginning to feel the sense of being hemmed in, had been on the point of making a *volte-face*, of swivelling round completely and bounding towards Pulpit Gap behind him as fast as he could, aware that he would be running straight into the danger behind him but trusting to his speed to carry him through it. But the sudden increase in noise at his back made him change his mind. There might be more danger there than he knew about. Already fear, like a little dark cloud, was beginning to make itself felt in his brain, clouding his judgement and upsetting his decisions. *He was hunted.*

It was this that made him compromise. With a sudden contemptuous and angry toss of his heavily antlered head he turned and made off.

But he didn't turn completely. He turned through a half-circle. He was suspicious of the woods in front and now beginning to be scared of Man behind him, so he compromised and ran to the side, making for a part of the wood with which he was not very familiar.

Robert knew it well enough and he could have wished that His Lordship had not chosen to head that way. But this was better, at least, than seeing him break back to Pulpit Gap.

' Come on, Jack,' he cried, for quiet was now not even desirable. ' We mun keep the old devil a-going now.'

As he ran he let out a third owl's cry—an unconvincing one this time, for it was a difficult thing to do on the move, but he hoped the hot-headed young Norman and the boy would guess its import.

They did ; and seeing the hunt to be up in good earnest they both increased their speed, making heavy going of it in the coarse grass.

As yet the stag was only trotting. It was a movement he performed with infinite grace and lightness, and watching him you could hardly have believed him to be the heavy powerful creature that he was.

The running stag and the running man—there could be no comparison between them in grace and power. Nor was there any comparison between the inside of their heads. As the stag trotted he thought after a fashion, it is true ; but it was only confused thinking, composed principally of fear telling him to get away.

As man was running, as Robert the hunter was running, he was thinking much more incisively than that.

He was thinking about what his quarry would do. From the way the woods curved and from the position of the boy and the Norman, it seemed likely to Robert that the stag would swing left-handed when he gained the trees ; the more so as there was a very marshy patch of ground there, and instinct would send him to the water to smother his scent.

' Let him turn then,' Robert thought, and he halted, throwing up a hand and calling to Jack Wildman to bring him up short too.

Jack was blowing hard ; he carried twenty years more than the other man, to say nothing of an extra two stones in weight.

' Bide a bit, Jack, bide a bit. Let 'un turn if 'un wants to and come back a bit towards us. If we can get a score of yards farther on we might get a shot at 'un yet.'

Jack nodded, content to leave the leadership to the younger man.

' Mortal good job the old devil didn't run for the Gap,' he whispered, still drawing breath hard.

Robert grinned. ' I warrant we'll need a pint or two time we get back,' he answered. ' Fit your shaft and follow me. Time we get to Fenny Ride I reckon we're as likely to get a look at His Lordship as not.'

136

Jack fitted an arrow into the half-ready position and followed Robert, who, now moving very cautiously but fairly quickly, was walking forward again. It was rough going, for they had gained the trees once more and in the pools of darkness, where the foliage denied the moonlight, it was hard to tell what was underfoot. But presently Robert held up his hand again, and the two men halted on the edge of a broad ride where the green grass lay miraculously silvered by moonshine.

They took cover behind two medium-sized oaks and listened.

What Robert hoped was that the other two, the boy and Rufus the Norman, had continued running and so by the scare of their noise, if by nothing else, had denied the far right-hand corner of the wood to the stag. If they had, and if His Lordship had decided to turn left-handed through the marshy part to help smother his scent, he would likely enough emerge into Fenny Ride before long.

And that would be the moment, Robert knew, for action.

As soon as the quarry came into sight they must take their shot at him.

Miss him *here* and they might well miss him for good, because he would be off down the broad avenue of Fenny Ride like the wind, and they might as well all go whistling home. So Robert touched Jack on the arm (he judged it dangerous to talk now) and moved his bow slightly to show what was in his mind. Wildman nodded and grinned. He understood perfectly. He got his own bow ready and looked in the moonlight to make certain that it was his favourite shaft flighted with the goose feathers that he had fitted to it.

Thus they waited. Each man now on one knee, the perfect position from which to draw a hunting bow ; each man. straining eye and ear, acutely aware of every tiny half-noise of the night, and of the confusing, bewildering intermingling of sharp moonlight and deep black shadow under the trees on the far side of the ride.

These were moments of pure joy for Robert the hunter. Mere, sheer, uncomplicated joy of existence. This was what he loved—the hunt and the climax of it. For the moment it mattered nothing to him that what he was doing meant his death if he was discovered ; he couldn't even think of that, for the moment. All he could think about, straining eyes and ears to their sharpest uttermost, was whether his guess would be right and where his quarry would first appear.

Six minutes may have passed like this, perhaps even longer ; a long time when a man is keyed-up and afraid almost to breathe. Then Robert made something which was too small to be called a noise through his nostrils. It was a tiny suggestion of sound just sufficient to warn the man by his side.

For three seconds Jack could see nothing ; then he spotted it too.

From between two large oak-trees on the far side on the ride, and moving now from the shadow of the trees into the silvery moonlight of the ride itself, came the big stag. He was walking. It looked as though he had been somewhat reassured by the lessening of noise behind him and by the comfort of coming through the water of the marshy patch. When he gained the edge of the ride he halted for a moment in full moonlight and stood there looking what he was : the king of the woodlands.

Jack swallowed hard and raised his bow into position. One goose feather of the shaft brushed asperously against his cheek as he drew and steadied himself for the necessary moment. He supposed Robert was doing the same ; but he didn't really think about it. He didn't really think about anything except the shaft and the bent bow and the thing he was aiming at.

The stag was within easy bow-shot, and when it moved its head as though giving warning that it intended to start walking again, Jack tugged his shaft-end back the extra bit and let fly.

He missed ; he saw his shaft go wide in the moonlight and cursed quickly and angrily under his breath, as any man will who aims at any mark and fails to hit it.

But it didn't matter all that much, for Robert the hunter hadn't missed.

He had loosed his shaft at precisely the same instant. It was a shade heavier than Jack's, although it came from a lighter bow, and it sped true and unerring into its deadly work. It struck the stag in the thick of his neck, just above the shoulder, and he let out a bellow of indignation, hurt and fright. For a moment he went up in the air, rearing almost like a horse ; then, when he came down, he flung round and made off into the tangle of trees behind him.

'Got 'un, got 'un,' cried Robert delightedly. This was just what he wanted. Could hardly be better. He knew the shaft had gone well home and that the stag must already be losing blood ; on top of which the beast would be scared and would blunder about among the trees instead of making use of his speed in the open.

'Come on, Jack, come on.' Robert was half-way across the ride already, and Jack was after him chanting, 'Leu, leu, leu' under his breath and hoping desperately that he could get the chance of another shot.

Away, beyond, the boy and the Norman heard the bellow of the stag and interpreted it rightly. He had been hit and now anything might happen. They increased their pace as best they could through the trees ; and when the stag turned and ran from what he now perceived to be mortal danger in front of him, the boy, running up from behind, came face to face with him for a moment.

The beast was bewildered now. There was danger before

and behind, whichever way he turned. With an agility amazing in a beast of his size and weight he jerked to the left and bounded away among the trees.

'Forrard, forrard,' Robert cried urgently, of necessity throwing all caution to the wind now. 'Spread, spread. Get 'un moithered. Turn 'un, turn 'un.'

This was the hunter's game and Robert was adroit at it. Under his direction, partly by skill and partly also by the luck which must attend any hunting episode to make it successful, they managed to do what they aimed at. Between them the four of them (aided by Snapper who ran mute but tireless) kept heading the now thoroughly bewildered stag and turning him back until he didn't know how much danger there was or where it threatened most. The whole forest seemed full of enemies to the poor beast; he was frightened and all the time he was losing blood. He had brushed close enough to a tree trunk to snap off the shaft of the arrow that had hit him, but the savage head of it was still embedded in his neck muscles, and blood was running freely.

All this counted in the favour of the men hunting him; but not everything had gone in their favour by any means. Something not far short of tragedy had overtaken Jack Wildman, who had fallen into an old saw pit. It had been dug in the woods a generation before when some oaks had been felled, and had lain there, deceptively overgrown by bracken and grass, ever since.

Jack didn't hurt himself, having almost as much knack as a wild thing in falling soft, but—*snap*. He heard it go under him. His bow. He left it there, cursing as hard as he could. A good bow was not a thing you came by easily; and now they had only Robert's to rely on for the night's work.

And Robert, after that first good true shot of his, made a bad blunder.

Out of the confusion and turmoil of running and counter-running ; of stopping to listen ; of making sudden noises to confuse the stag ; of long silences, a moment came, just as, by experience, he knew it would, when by sheer luck he got the chance of a shot.

It was a longer draw than the first, but still well within bow-shot, and Robert didn't hesitate. The first shaft had been broken off, he noticed, but he could see that the head was still there and that most of the stag's forehand now glistened in the moonlight, showing that plenty of blood was still running.

' Good, good,' thought Robert. Another shaft well home and the work would be nearing its end.

Without hesitation he sank on one knee, fitted one of his two remaining arrows, and drew.

It was a bad shot. He should have remembered that when a man has been running backwards and forwards in thick undergrowth for some twenty minutes his breath is apt to come a bit jerkily and his hands are likely to shake a little. He drew too quickly and his shot jinked wide. It embedded itself three inches into the solid wood of a living oak-tree and stuck there quivering in the moonlight.

' God A'mighty, if that had hit 'un, he'd have knowed about it,' Robert thought. But it hadn't hit ; and now they were down to one arrow only. He didn't even waste time trying to recover the other one from the bole of the oak. He knew what the head of it would be like. An arrow had to be in perfect trim to be of any use at all, and one that had buried itself in the bole of an oak would want a deal of attention from the fletcher before it was usable again.

The stag, startled by the noise of the arrow striking the tree close by, started to run again ; and cursing, Robert ran after it. Five minutes later he got the chance of another shot and didn't know what to do about it.

It wasn't the easiest of shots, yet it was a definite chance.

But then, again, it was his last arrow and it might be as well to reserve it for something nearer the end. He had to make up his mind quickly; and still stung by annoyance at his recent bad miss, he fitted the shaft, drew it in careful aim, and let fly.

He could tell by the bellow the stag gave that the arrow had gone home, although he couldn't see where before the beast turned and bounded off again.

Robert grinned. That made up to some extent for his miss. Two wounds now, so surely the great old devil would begin to tire soon.

He did. That second shaft of Robert's had all but missed. It caught the stag, not in any vital body part, but low down in his left leg—a wound which was vital in this sense, that it slowed him up at once. Running was now an exceedingly painful business for him; and more than ever fear mounted within him.

He gave up running and for the first time turned at bay; and so, still closing relentlessly in on him, the four men found him standing in a shallow stream where the cold of the water eased the pain in his leg.

His great chest was flecked with foam and blood; blood was darkening the water that he stood in; his nostrils were widely dilated with hard-taken breath and with fear; and fear showed in his distended eyes.

'In, Snapper, in,' Robert urged; and Snapper needed no urging. He went in swiftly and unheedingly.

He would have done better to be more circumspect. The stag had been run by a hound before, and knew something about them. As fast as a fencer at play of sword he lowered his head, caught the oncoming hound on the cruel sharpness of an antler, and with a mighty upward jerk of his powerful neck muscles sent him flying, to land twenty feet away with blood pouring from a wound in his punctured belly. The end of Snapper.

It looked like being the end of the stag too. With a sudden convulsive effort he scrambled up the bank behind him, sending a shower of stones and earth into the stream. Then, having gained a place on top of the bank, he stood swaying for a moment or two as though the effort of getting up there had been the last thing he could manage, and fell heavily : first on to his knees, then sideways on to his flank.

The four slower, weaker, but more cunning animals who had brought the great beast to this sorry pass stood their distance, watching.

Robert, who had seen the death agonies of many a stag, was just thinking : ' Give 'un five minutes and 'twill be safe to go in,' when, to his consternation and dismay, he saw the young Norman Rufus de Burgh rushing forward.

' Hold hard ! ' Robert shouted. ' Hold hard, man ! '

But in vain. Rufus thought the stag was either dead or so near it as to make no difference. He felt that hitherto he had done nothing to distinguish himself in the chase and that it was up to him, a Norman, and a de Burgh at that, at least to show the Saxon hinds that he had no fear in the matter. And indeed he had no fear. He was young and in the prime of condition and completely exhilarated by the excitement of the chase.

Drawing his short knife from its leather case at his hip he suddenly rushed forward, stumbled through the stream, and, dripping water from his knees downwards, scrabbled up the high bank on the far side.

' *Hold hard !* ' he heard the Saxon hind cry warningly, but young Rufus merely laughed in his strength, and shouted out the Norman hunting cry : ' Ohe, ohe ! '

He ran to where the stag lay and seized hold of its antlers, intending to shift the head slightly to one side so as to get a better aim for plunging in his short, dagger-like knife.

' God and all His saints ! ' Robert cried, watching, for the young Norman had hardly so much as touched the stag's antlers before the great beast sprang up.

It was as though a dead thing had suddenly come to life again.

With a bellow of anger the stag reared up, tossing his noble head high and actually lifting Rufus up on his antlers.

The Norman realized his danger now, but the first upward blow of those savage horns had knocked all the wind out of him and for a second or two he could do nothing. The stag, still carrying this fantastic burden on its head, stumbled backwards, at the same time slewing round to one side. Rufus began to slip down towards the ground and was now desperately trying to get his knife to work.

Back again the stag went ; and this time back too far. The patch of ground where this last strange encounter was being enacted stood on the very edge of an old, deep chalk pit. The final convulsive effort of the animal took its hindquarters over the edge ; and now, plunge and scrabble frantically though it might, it could do nothing to save itself, and stag and man, still locked in struggle, toppled over and went sliding, rolling, and crashing twenty feet down into the pit.

The noise of this desperate end to everything died away completely, and for a few seconds the wood was quiet again before anything else happened.

Then Robert ran quickly forward, and hard on his heels Jack Wildman and the boy followed.

It had been such a splendid thing to watch, that for the moment the boy felt nothing but exhilaration. But the two Saxon men felt something very different. Together they knelt over the side of the chalk pit and peered down into it. The moonlight did not reach right to the bottom, but it was just possible to make out two forms lying in the water there.

' De Burgh, de Burgh,' Robert cried urgently.

No answer came up from the pit, nor was there any movement.

'*De Burgh!*' Jack Wildman called, as though his voice might somehow be heard when the other man's wasn't.

But no voice was heard, and Jack Wildman, too, went unanswered.

Robert straightened up a little and sank back on his haunches.

'Stag's dead,' he said, 'and the Norman too by the looks of it—the powerful young fool.'

Jack Wildman nodded.

'And what next?' he asked almost in a whisper.

The two men stared at one another in the moonlight; and the boy, watching their faces, was fascinated. All the excitement of the chase had gone and fear was beginning to take its place.

Robert was thinking hard. This was a kettle of fish that he didn't want to have anything to do with at all. Poaching had been bad enough; but there was always a chance with poaching that you might get away without paying the extremest penalty of the law. A dead Norman was a very different matter.

To have anything to do with a dead Norman meant that the three of them would be hanged, with the fewest possible questions asked and with the least possible delay in time. And not only would they be hanged but in all probability vengeance would be taken on their families as well. Duke William didn't like Saxon churls killing his Norman gentlemen.

Robert knew this; Jack Wildman knew it; to a lesser extent even the boy knew it. The knowledge had been burnt and branded into the Saxon consciousness by twenty years of iron rule.

Robert rose to his feet, and when he spoke it was in a whisper.

'We'd best get out of here and quickly,' he said. 'Even if they find this young Norman fool here in the pit—*who shall know who was with him ?*'

Wildman nodded ; he was thinking hard.

'Snapper ?' he asked.

'Any one's hound. Who knows he was mine ? Not the Normans, anyway. They haven't got that down in their damned great book, have they ?'

'And the shafts, if they find them ?'

'Mine carry no mark. Do yours ?'

'No.'

'What then ? Home, lads, and keep your mouths shut. Don't forget ; what isn't told can't be found out. Know nothing and say nothing. Not to anybody.'

He turned and started to move. He knew, and the other two with him knew, that the urgent thing now was to get away from the spot ; to get out of the wood and back to their homes before any one saw them.

So they wasted no time. Robert the hunter went in front, setting the pace ; Jack Wildman and the boy followed.

There was an odd turmoil of thoughts in the boy's head. He felt suddenly deflated, like a blown-up pig's bladder when the air is let out of it quickly. The night had been charged with the exhilaration of pure excitement, so sharp and sweet that all else—time, danger, whereabouts—had been forgotten ; and now suddenly that was all gone and fear was in its place. Fear, and, in the boy's mind at least, something else. A little nagging hint of unhappiness. Suppose young Rufus de Burgh was *not* quite dead ; suppose he was injured, lying there unconscious in the pit, in danger of slipping down into the stagnant water in the bottom and drowning. . . .

'Hurry,' Robert called quietly over his shoulder. 'Every yard counts.'

He had already led them out of the wood, and before long

147

they would be back at the outskirts of the village. At that time of the night they did not expect to meet anybody; and they certainly did not want to.

Once they were back in their homes they were safe, for there would be three households willing to swear that none of them had ever left withindoors all evening.

The very first building of the village was a crude stone affair, built originally as a barn, but now disused and falling to pieces. It threw a hard black shadow across the grassy track they were on, and here they halted, for their ways must diverge.

Robert said : 'Home now, all of us, as quick as we can. Remember : we've not seen one another this night; nor been out of our houses. Least said, soonest mended. Say nothing and there's nothing to mend. And damn me if ever I take a Norman hunting again; red deer or anything else. 'Twas a fool's game to start with.'

He turned, and, walking by the long side of the old barn, made off.

Jack Wildman's way to the mill lay to the left, and he waited only long enough to say a couple of words.

'Robert's right, young 'un,' he said.

'I know it, Jack. You don't think I shall be blabbing about it, do you?'

'No, I don't. You've too much sense for one thing. Pity we didn't get the venison.'

'There are always other nights.'

'Not for me,' Jack answered, laughing. 'I reckon I'm getting too old for this sort of game. I'll turn honest and take to prayers.' And with a laugh he too was gone, humming a bit under his breath, for he reckoned the danger had gone by now; and the boy was left alone.

He knew already what he was going to do. Although he began to go straight on automatically (for that was the way to the cott where his family lived) he knew quite well in his heart that he was going to do something different. There was a very vivid image running strongly in his mind, and by its intensity compelling him to turn back.

He was thinking all the time of young Rufus de Burgh's smiling, friendly face ; of the grace of him and the charm. Something had passed between them when they had smiled at one another ; it was as though either of them, or it could have been both, had said the words : ' We are young together, you and I. Not Saxon or Norman, but young English friends on English soil. Never let it be different.'

And with this memory of the young Norman's friendly smile went also the disturbing thought : ' Maybe he isn't dead. Maybe he is lying hurt at the bottom of the pit, wanting help.'

So from the beginning when Jack Wildman had left him and gone humming off towards Do-little Mill it had been inevitable ; and the boy had not gone a slow hundred yards in the direction of his home before he halted, turned, and, quickening his pace almost to a trot, began to retrace his steps.

He hurried, partly because he realized that he was in danger every moment until the night's work was over, partly because he thought that if Rufus needed help he probably needed it badly—*now*.

He hadn't Robert the hunter's expert and extensive know-ledge of the wood and he got lost a little and went out of his way. But that was soon put right ; and it wasn't very long before he was back at the pit edge again. Just as he was bending down he was startled by the long-drawn cry of an owl. His nerves were so taut that he jerked his head up in unreasoning alarm for a moment, Robert and the hunt and all the urgency and danger of the evening crowding in on him.

Then he realized that this *was* an owl and not Robert

any longer, and he gave a laugh and shrugged off his fears and applied himself to the work in hand. He bent over the pit edge and, peering down into the darkness below, called :

'De Burgh, Rufus, ohe ! Are you there ? '

Something which might have been a groan, or a grunt, or an answer of some sort floated back to him, and his heart sang. At any rate it was a noise, a human noise, and Rufus de Burgh was alive.

'Are you hurt ? ' he called. 'Badly ? '

The noise came again ; no more intelligible, but still something. The boy let himself over the edge of the pit and began to descend it cautiously. It wasn't easy to keep either foot- or hand-hold, and he slithered the last few feet, arriving at the bottom with a bump.

His eyes took five seconds to get accustomed to the darkness down there and then he began to make out things. He was almost standing on the stag, which had broken a leg in its fall and was lying in an ungainly huddle. It had bled freely in its death throes and there was a deal of blood about in consequence. Lying close to the stag, and with the lower half of him already in the water which filled the bottom of the pit, was the young Norman.

He had been badly stunned by the fall, catching his head on a stone and knocking all the senses out of himself ; and he had lost a good deal of blood from a wound in his face caused by the stag's antlers, with the result that he had only just recovered consciousness and felt sick and lightheaded. But he was alive, and when the boy bent over him and spoke he knew who it was.

'Are you badly hurt ? ' the boy asked.

'No. I don't think so. I must have hit my head or something.' The voice was still thick and uncertain, but it was getting better already.

The boy made what examination he could of the injuries to head and face. They were unpleasant, but they didn't look to him to be desperately bad. The urgency for them both to get away was still on him.

' Can you move ? ' he asked.

Rufus de Burgh struggled to a sitting position with an effort and a grunt. He had broken a collar-bone by his fall, but he was not, specifically, aware of this. He merely knew that all over him he felt one large aching pain. But things were clearing rapidly in his head now and life was beginning to reassert itself.

He tried to laugh, and found the pain in his cheek excruciatingly painful for a moment.

' *Ah*.'

' You're bad ? '

' No. Not really. I shall move all right in a minute or two. The stag's dead ? '

The boy kicked the beast at his side.

' And a miracle you're not too,' he said.

' Ay,' de Burgh kept his face straight because of his torn cheek, but laughed in his voice, and the boy knew he must be getting better.

' Can you give me a hand ? ' Rufus asked. ' I think I could get up.'

The boy helped him, and Rufus got to his feet and leant against the side of the pit. The effort of rising made him feel dizzy again and he shut his eyes. But it was only a momentary set-back ; and now that he was upright and on his feet his head began to feel better at once.

He put his hand up to his cheek.

' The old devil caught me in the face,' he said, ' but I reckon the blood's stopped running now.'

' You went in at him too soon.'

' Ay. I see that—now.' This time he did manage to

laugh, and it was not quite so painful. He looked upwards into the moonlight, estimating the climb up the pit side.

'Can you help me up, think you?' he asked.

'Surely. Look, Rufus, get on to that ledge half-way up, if you can; then if you wait there whilst I get to the top I can pull you up the rest of the way.'

De Burgh nodded. 'But don't pull too hard,' he begged. 'I feel as though a horse had rolled on me.'

It was not a difficult matter to get him on to the narrow ledge of earth and rock that jutted out half-way up one side; but the effort of getting there made him puff a good deal, and he was glad to have to rest whilst the boy found a different route up to the top.

'All right?' the boy asked, hanging over the pit edge, and reaching down with his arms.

'Ay. But gently, gently.'

Gently it was; and gently did it. And, without too much strain or distress, the boy had him out presently and they faced one another in the moonlight, both kneeling.

Young de Burgh got to his feet, unaided this time, and tested himself with tentative stretchings and reachings.

'Better?' the boy asked.

De Burgh managed to laugh again.

'All of one piece,' he answered. 'Except that one shoulder feels a little strange. I wouldn't want to take part in a tournament yet.'

'Can you walk?'

'Yes, surely, I can walk.' De Burgh took a few steps to prove it and then fetched up short. 'But where are the others?' he asked, looking about him in a puzzled way.

'Gone.'

'Gone? How, where?'

'Home. I went with them, but I came back.'

'How long since I fell into the pit with the stag, then?'

152

The boy considered. He could judge time easily during the day if he had sight of the sun, not so easily otherwise.

'It must be almost an hour,' he said.

'*Almost an hour?*'

'Not far from it by now.'

'But—but—I thought it was three minutes or so. Five at the most.'

The boy laughed. 'Your head was hurt,' he pointed out.

'Ay. No doubt. But it is clearer now. Still—an hour! And the other two have gone home, leaving me?'

'They thought you were dead, and were afraid.'

Young de Burgh nodded. He understood all the implications of the situation perfectly, and felt not the slightest resentment against the two Saxon men. In their case he would have done precisely the same.

'You'll not hold it against them—say anything?' the boy asked.

'Say anything? By the Holy Cross, no. We all went out after the deer together. I liked them both, Robert and the other one. It was my fault the thing went wrong. I'll say nothing, my round oath on it, except a tale of running and a fall and not remembering.'

'Good, good, I thought you would be like that. They wouldn't have gone off except for the Laws, and thinking you were dead——'

'You thought I was dead, too?'

'Yes, in a way. And in a way, no. I wasn't sure. I thought you might only be hurt.'

'So you came back?'

'I came back, Rufus.'

'To help me?'

'If you were not dead you would want help, I told myself.'

'A Saxon to help a Norman, eh?'

'Come on,' the boy urged, 'we shall not be clear till we are each safely home again. Can you walk, think you?'

'Ay. I can walk. I'm coming; but first—' he held out his right hand, and after a moment's hesitation the boy took it in his, and so the two young men stood facing one another in the moonlight.

'I'll remember this night's work,' Rufus de Burgh said. 'Always. Some day if you want help, come to me and then you shall find that we are of one blood, and a Norman shall help a Saxon.'

Their two right hands gripped one another, and the boy was warm and happy with a great feeling of friendship.

Then a cloud began to obscure the moon and the light failed suddenly. Failed until de Burgh and the space they stood in and the trees beyond were misted over and disappeared. . . .

.   .   .   .   .

The boy found himself staring up at the beech-tree.

'Cunning little beggar,' he thought as the squirrel disappeared from sight. 'I bet he's watching me from somewhere.'

He stepped over the stile and began to walk across Street Meadow towards the bottom of the Doctor's garden.

When he got there Albert Wilde had just arrived.

'See where the old Manor stood, Mus' Tom?' he inquired.

Tom passed his hand over his forehead quickly. 'There's really nothing left of it now, is there?' he asked.

'Nothing left of anything,' Albert chuckled, ''cept this mortal celery, and I shall be in a packet of trouble if I don't get on with 'ee.'

PART THREE

PILGRIMS

(English : A.D. 1360)

'TIMBER hates all this gauzy tulle stuff,' Eleanor said, feeling that she must say something to excuse the misbehaviour of her dearly beloved pony, who was doing pretty well everything short of a full-blooded buck in an effort to show that he thoroughly disapproved of the whole proceeding.

The whole proceeding was, in fact, nothing less than a rehearsal for the Mounted Fancy Dress Parade at the forthcoming Gymkhana organized by the Pony Club.

'Let's go as a band of Arabs,' Jump had suggested when the three of them had decided to enter, and were then faced with the always awkward question : what were they to dress up as ?

'A band of Arabs ?' Eleanor said scornfully. 'What a perfectly foul idea !'

'I call it a jolly good idea,' Jennifer said quickly and loyally. She often found it necessary to side with little Jump against their lordly elder sister.

'Well, you think of something better,' Jump put in, adding

157

quickly, because the idea had just occurred to him, and it was a passion of his at the moment—'pirates perhaps?'

'Pirates on horseback?' Eleanor said, 'don't be silly. We'd want a boat if we were going to be pirates.'

'P'raps we could have a boat,' Jump said dreamily. He loved boats.

'That's just plain potty,' Jennifer put in decisively and promptly. Jennifer was the matter-of-fact, sensible one of the two, and what she said usually went in the end. 'A band of Arabs is a jolly good idea,' she went on, 'and I vote we do it and get some stuff from Mum's jumble-sale drawer, and practise it this afternoon.'

That settled it; and there they were, all three of them in Street Meadow, practising being a Band of Arabs. Tom was in attendance on foot, acting as stage-manager, audience, and critic, and thoroughly enjoying himself.

Jennifer was riding Cinders, a well-bred, narrow-backed little thing, dainty in all her movements and much too well-behaved to make a fuss about anything, even if she didn't like it very much.

Jump, aged eight, sat sturdily and squarely on his dependable Polly, who had a back like a kitchen-table and would cheerfully have trotted through the worst traffic in Piccadilly and never turned a hair.

It was only Timber who was playing up. And as Timber, a flaunting, flouncing nervy chestnut, always played up, nobody paid very much attention.

The jumble-sale drawer was a completely invaluable storehouse whenever Charades, Pageants, or Fancy Dress of any kind had to be coped with; and once again it had not failed them. Mrs Mason had protested a bit; but the protestations of Mum were like the Admonitions of Teachers: you listened politely to what was said and then took no notice of it whatsoever. All the children quite understood that grown-ups just had to protest about pretty well everything; it was in their nature.

The jumble-sale drawer yielded yards of green tulle (the stuff to which Timber took such a rooted objection); several scarves of different colours; and a queer assortment of footwear.

'I'm jolly sure Arabs never wore boots like these,' Jump said.

'Never mind,' Jennifer told him, 'nobody will know. I bet you nobody in Dallicombe has ever seen an Arab.'

'Let's do some jumps,' Eleanor suggested.

'Arabs don't jump.'

'Who says?'

'What would there be to jump over in the desert?'

'This isn't a desert, it's Street Meadow. Put the jump up, Tom.'

Tom laughed and walked towards the low, home-made jump of two boards and some gorse between, which was lying on the ground. Personally he didn't mind whether they jumped their ponies or simply rode round; it was all one to him; he loved just being in Street Meadow.

The little jump had been lying on its side for some time and one end of it had got lodged into the hedge at the side of the field. Tom had to bend down and tug pretty hard to get it free.

'Pull hard,' Eleanor urged him.

Tom pulled hard; and the end of the jump came loose unexpectedly, bringing a briar out of the hedge whipping back with it, so that Tom jerked back his head and instinctively shut his eyes.

.   .   .   .   .

When he had opened them again and had brushed his hand quickly across his face to get rid of the quick little stinging pain, the young man riding at his side laughed sympathetically and said:

159

'These springy bushes are the devil, aren't they?'

They were riding together through a narrow neck of woodland; and the boy knew that his companion's name was Geoffrey. They had been together for the whole day.

'The point about going through this bit of woodland,' Geoffrey went on, 'is that it's a short cut to the old road that leads down to the town—there, you can see where the road goes now.'

They had reached the edge of the woodland, and both reined their horses for a moment to look out over the meadow with the little stream in it and the flat width of green running beside.

'Grassed over now,' Geoffrey said, 'and has been these thousand years or more, I don't doubt. Green-roads I call 'em, and you can find scores of them, hundreds I expect, all over England. Good for riding on. Firm but not too hard on the nags' feet.'

'You've ridden far in England?' the boy asked a little enviously, a little admiringly, because although he was seventeen years old, he himself, as it chanced, had not travelled far, and this business of going on pilgrimage was something of an adventure for him.

But Geoffrey, three years older, had already done fantastic things like going to France only the previous year to join King Edward's train and being taken prisoner and then ransomed.

He laughed—he was always laughing—and *chk-chk-ed* with his tongue to tell his yellow, unhandy horse to get moving again.

'I've been about a bit,' he agreed. 'This is the second time I've been on this pilgrimage affair.'

'I wouldn't have thought you were all that holy,' the boy teased him; and Geoffrey narrowed his lively dark eyes— a trick of his when amused—and laughed again loudly.

'I'm not holy, I'm afraid,' he said. 'I'm human. On a trip like this you get all sorts and conditions of people. Men and women, both. And I just love to ride along with them and study them.'

'Have you been studying me then, Geoffrey?'

'Ay. As a monk does his book. No, "study" is too dusty a word. I mean it's fun to be with other human beings and to find out what they're like, and where they all come from, and what they do.'

They were interrupted by young Sir Thomas, who rode back from the head of the little company of thirty people, who, in twos and threes and sometimes one at a time, on allsorts and conditions of horses, were strung along Street Meadow, heading down the valley.

Young Sir Thomas was better mounted than any of the others, or at least more showily so; and even towards the end of a long day's journeying his chestnut with the three white socks had plenty to say for itself.

As he rode up, Geoffrey said in an undertone: 'I wouldn't put it past that wild-looking thing of his to put in a couple of quick bucks and land him on the floor.'

'I wish it would,' the boy said, feeling a shade mean as he said it—because, after all, the worst fault you could find with young Sir Thomas was that he had a touch of the arrogance of youth about him.

His father, old Sir Thomas, was always referred to by everybody as The Knight, because he was one of the first men in England to be given the new honour of the Order of the Garter, which Edward had instituted only eleven years earlier.

Old Sir Thomas, who, for all his distinctions and decorations, was wearing a plain fustian tunic which showed dark stains where his armour had rubbed it, rode steadily and soberly at the head of the small band; and he sometimes turned an amused and tolerant eye on the caperings and noisy antics of his boy.

Young Sir Thomas wore no plain and metal-stained fustian.

'Just look at the embroidery on that cotte of his,' Geoffrey said under his breath.

'And the width of those sleeves!'

'You'd think he was going to court instead of riding on a pilgrimage.'

Young Sir Thomas was abreast of them now and he turned his horse to go along with theirs.

'Your nags look used up,' he said in his offhand way.

'We can't all afford thoroughbreds,' Geoffrey reminded him easily.

'You've travelled this road before, haven't you?'

'Once. Two, three years ago now, just before I went into France to join the King's train. My father was all against my going off to the war against the French. As a matter of fact he's against the whole French war——'

'Against the French war?' young Sir Thomas cried incredulously. 'Why should the Frenchmen do what they like with our lands over there? And what's a gentleman to do if he doesn't fight, anyway?'

'But my father isn't a gentleman,' Geoffrey retorted softly. 'He's a vintner of the City of London.'

'Well, that's profitable, I'll warrant.'

'As long as you don't go to war with the people you buy the wine from,' Geoffrey pointed out.

The boy, listening to them both, laughed out loud at this. He didn't know which of them had the right of it. War was exciting, trade was profitable, so what was a young man to do?

'But you went to France in spite of your father?' he asked.

'Ay. I did. I told him I was going, too. Which was the cause of my first coming on this trip. "If you must go and give some good Burgundian the chance of splitting your silly young head open," my father told me, "for heaven's sake do a pilgrimage first and earn a bit of grace and goodness; and I'll pray for you every Sunday and holy day in St Martin-in-the-Vintry." That's our parish church in London. And that's how it was I did my first pilgrimage.'

'And you know the way?'

'Most of it. I've forgotten some.'

'Where do we lie tonight?'

Geoffrey pointed ahead down the small and homely valley.

'There's a town called Dalecombe,' he said, 'only a little place, but there's a good inn there. The Seven Stars.'

'How far off is this Dalecombe?'

'Not twenty minutes if we walk—and that's all my nag wants to do this time of day.'

'You should give him more corn and less hay. What's the sport in Dalecombe?' asked young Sir Thomas.

'We sit by the fireside in the Seven Stars,' Geoffrey answered seriously, 'and listen to the oldest inhabitant telling tales.'

'Marvellous sport, I'll warrant. No games? No ladies to be entertained?'

'You want Westminster or Winchester, young Sir Thomas. This is the sleepy country here, not your fashionable court. Though if it comes to that, I'd as soon sit and listen to your father, The Knight, tell a tale as I would do anything else. *He's* knocked about a bit and no mistake.'

Young Sir Thomas didn't enjoy the suggestion that anybody might be more interesting than himself. 'I could tell a pretty good yarn, if it comes to that,' he protested.

'Ay. I don't doubt it,' Geoffrey answered sweetly, 'but,

you see, the difference is that I should believe your father's tale and I'm not at all sure that I should believe yours.'

For a moment young Sir Thomas looked at him sharply and a quick, quarrelling word trembled on his lip. But Geoffrey's easy, good-natured smile disarmed the young squire, and he had the sense to check himself. He gave a quick nod of his head and, touching the chestnut with his heels, moved up towards the head of the company again.

The other two laughed, watching him go ; and the boy, curious as always about the great world and the exciting things to be seen and done in it, asked :

'What was it like in France at the wars ? What happened ?'

Geoffrey laughed. 'I don't mind telling you,' he said. 'But, believe me, if ever I had to tell the tale in public I should dress it up a bit differently. There were only twenty of us ; most of them were the Earl of Warwick's men, all wearing the Bear and the Ragged Staff, and we were told we were to join the Black Prince somewhere. Not that we minded very much exactly where we were off to. We lay in quarters in Dover for two days, waiting for a reasonable wind ; and we sang songs, and drank anything we could get hold of, and swapped yarns, and I won a shilling from a Warwickshire man at backgammon. Have you ever sailed the narrow seas from Dover ?'

'No, never. What's it like ?'

'I was a better Christian for having done it. I knew what hell was like. "Don't worry," the sailors told us when we got on shipboard at last, "it's only a bit choppy." By Saint Christopher, if that's what they call a bit choppy, I'll be hanged before I go to sea when it's rough. I didn't know anybody could be as sick as I was and not die. Long before we got to the French coast I didn't care about King Edward, or the Black Prince, or England, or France, or anything, except lying down against a coil of rope I had discovered, and shutting my eyes and praying for it all to end somehow.'

The boy laughed aloud.

'Poor you,' he said, 'what a start!'

Geoffrey laughed. 'I soon got over it, though.' He touched the boy on the arm and said: 'Just look at that sorry nag the Oxford scholar is riding. If that lasts out the whole journey I'll be surprised. You can see all its ribs now.'

'And the scholar's, too, I wouldn't wonder.'

'Moral: don't go up to Oxford in search of learning if you want to wax fat.'

'I'm not likely to,' the boy said, laughing. 'But tell me about the war.'

'Well, that's the silly part of it. There wasn't any war really as far as I'm concerned. We landed near a place called Boulogne, where the first thing I did was to sleep for ten hours solid. When I woke up I was as hungry as a hunter and felt absolutely all right again. Then we started marching to join up with the Black Prince. We did nothing but march. I didn't know roads could be so long or so straight. We didn't do any scrapping; there wasn't anybody to scrap with. I suppose we looked a pretty tough gang of chaps, all sticking together as we made our way through the villages, and the farmers just didn't argue. They let us lie up in the barns for the night, and we got eggs and milk, or bread and wine given us in the morning, and they were only too glad to see the back of us when we moved on to the next place. I'm not saying how many chickens or geese we found occasion to pick up on the way, because we had one or two old hands with us, and, as they said, "a man had to live somehow if it was only by his wits."

'I must say I got to like France very much indeed, and the French people. So it didn't worry me that we couldn't find where the fighting was. Well, after about a fortnight of this

165

we found ourselves somewhere near a place called Rheims, and by all accounts we were getting a bit nearer where things were happening. Or so a jolly, fat wine merchant told us, in whose orchard six of us were spending the afternoon. He had a daughter, too, just as jolly and nearly as fat as he was himself—the sort of girl young Sir Thomas here would have made great eyes at. She kept bringing wine out to us in the orchard, and cracking jokes with us about our French, and trying to learn English words from us, and altogether it was very jolly.

' I think it must have been about four o'clock—I know it was baking hot, anyway—when we all decided to have an hour's sleep. We were going to march on farther that evening, and it seemed a good idea to get a bit of a rest first.

' So, with the sunshine filtering down through the apple-trees and the noise of a slip of a stream coming up from the end of the orchard, we yawned and curled up in the grass and slept. I remember just before dozing off thinking what a pleasant place the world was.

' The next thing I knew, someone was poking me in the ribs with his toe ; and when I woke up and rubbed my eyes and realized what was happening, there were a couple of whacking great chaps standing over me, carrying enough arms to fight a tournament all by themselves—and one of them was kicking me to wake me up, and telling me I was a prisoner of the King of France.'

' Good lord ! '

' Not very martial, was it ? I *was* a prisoner, too. We all were. No more orchards in the sunshine and bottles of wine and fat girls. They lodged us in Saint Elroy castle, which is not far from Rheims ; and I'll swear there isn't a damper, danker, darker, more foul-smelling place in Christendom.'

' What happened next ? '

'King Edward laid siege to Rheims—but without the help of fifteen of us lying in the dungeon of St Elroy castle. Maybe it was because we weren't there that he did so badly. Anyway, he *did* do badly, so he called off the Rheims affair and tried the same game on with Paris; with the same result. Last year didn't seem to be very lucky for Englishmen in France, somehow. When the siege of Paris failed they patched up a peace; but I don't doubt we shall be fighting one another again next year; and for the next hundred years, if it comes to that! Anyway, I and two others from St Elroy were ransomed.'

'How did you manage that?'

Geoffrey closed one of his lively dark eyes in a knowing wink. 'Young Sir Thomas isn't the only one with grand connections,' he said. 'My father may be only a wine merchant of the City of London, but wine merchants have their uses; and he was once chosen to be under-butler to the King, when His Majesty visited Southampton way back in 1348.'

'What does the under-butler do?'

Geoffrey laughed, and said:

'Well, the King's butler is a very grand person, a lord, of course. He wears the uniform and pockets the pay, and probably doesn't know a damned thing about wine anyway, except how to drink it. The under-butler has to make certain that the wine is there; that there's enough of it; that it's the right sort; and that it's good.

'My father could do that, all right, because what he doesn't know about wine you could tell whilst a priest gabbles a *Pater*. And he did it so well, and Edward was so pleased with him, that at the end of the Southampton visit the King sent for him and said: "Master Chaucer, if you ever find yourself out of employment, or wanting a favour, come you to court and remind me of what good management you made

167

of my wines here at Southampton, and I'll see what I can do for you." Which was a very pleasant thing to have said to you by the King—although my father didn't worry much about it, not being a court man but a London merchant, and knowing that it is the way of princes to be polite today and displeased tomorrow. But when news came to him that I was a prisoner, he bethought himself of what the King had said, and made application to the court.

'Of course, it was the usual story. He had to make things right with the Keeper of This and the Holder of That and the Custodian of Something Else before he could begin to hope of getting a message to the King himself. Still, that wasn't very difficult for father, who had plenty of bottles of good sherris sack to spare without too much cost to himself. So, to cut a long story short, in the end Edward himself paid sixteen pounds out of the royal purse towards my ransom, my father doubled it, and here I am, only too ready to go to Canterbury and thank Saint Thomas for my good luck.'

'What about the others in the castle of—where was it?'

'St Elroy. Two of them were ransomed with me, as I told you. The rest—' young Geoffrey Chaucer, aged twenty years and six months, shrugged his shoulders. 'God knows. The poor devils are still there, I should think, rotting away in the damp darkness, listening to the rats at night and notching up each hopeless day with a scratch on the wall. When you are a prisoner people forget your very existence.'

The boy shivered a little at the thought of that dark, dismal dungeon in far-away France, where maybe at that very moment a dozen Englishmen were eating their hearts out for their native Warwickshire. Cold though the evening air of the April day was, and heavy though the rainspots just beginning to fall might be, he was devoutly thankful to be out in it.

By this time they had come to the end of the green-road and were crowded together in the narrow lane into which it led.

168

The boy found himself jostling against the fat old lady from Bath, who, although they had been only a couple of days on the journey, already looked like dominating the proceedings. Secretly the boy thought she looked dreadful, with her over-raddled cheeks and her enormous hat, and the gap between her front teeth which showed up with ugly prominence when she smiled.

'God's day,' she shouted. She was slightly deaf herself and seemed to think that everybody else was too. 'I'll be pleased to reach wherever it is we're coming to and get off this nag of mine. I haven't ridden so much for years.'

The boy nodded and smiled. What he was really thinking was that in all probability the nag would be pleased too ; for Mistress Bath weighed every bit of eighteen stone in the saddle and was a most inexpert rider, of the sort that makes everything as hard as possible for the poor unfortunate mount.

'We shan't be long now, ma'am,' he answered politely. 'I can see a church spire, so that must mean the town's nigh.'

'You can keep the church,' the woman from Bath snapped peevishly. 'We've enough parsons and friars and nuns and what-not in the company as it is. What I want to see is no church but the inside of a good inn. I've been wet through three times today with these April showers, and I'm tired of it. What's the inn called ? '

'The Seven Stars,' Geoffrey put in from the other side.

'Eh ?'

'The Seven Stars,' Geoffrey repeated, shouting so loud that his horse jerked its head in alarm.

'All right, young man, all right. I'm not the breadth of England away. And what's it like, this Seven Stars of yours ? Clean and comfortable ? '

'I've slept in worse places.'

'That's but little recommendation. And the food ? '

'Let me see,' Geoffrey answered, half-shutting his lively

eyes and pretending that he was trying to remember. 'The last time I came this way and lodged here we had some stewed mutton ; boiled capon stuffed and with white sauce ; roasted pigeons ; and spiced cakes to end up with.'

The fat red face of Mistress Bath broke into a gap-toothed smile of satisfaction. 'That's worth a pilgrimage. That's the best news I've heard since we started out, young man.'

'Greedy old woman,' Geoffrey said as he pushed his horse on out of earshot. 'She'll be lucky if she gets a well-done coney. Hallo, what's all this ?'

They had reached the centre of the small, stone-built town of Dalecombe by now, and it was evident that something was afoot.

Three gaily painted wagons, such as the travelling showmen used, were drawn up close to the inn and a small crowd of children of all sorts and sizes stood silently staring at them in wonder and expectation.

A countryman clad in an old and much-worn leather jerkin was going by, and Geoffrey hailed him to find out what it was all about. The countryman had a weather-beaten, humorous face and was disposed to be friendly.

'Show people,' he answered, confirming what Geoffrey and the boy had already guessed. 'On the road from Exeter, so one of them tells me. They're going to give an entertainment tonight. Tumblers and a juggler and all such like. And they say there's a bear, but I haven't seen it. What with this lot and now you pilgrim people turning up, Dalecombe hasn't had as many people in it since Michaelmas Fair times before the pestilence came.'

Geoffrey smiled and nodded. 'I suppose all the town will turn out tonight ?' he asked.

'Sure to. 'Tisn't often we get a do of any sort. So don't you ladies and gentlemen on pilgrimage drink all the beer ; ploughing's thirsty work.'

'So is riding on pilgrimage.'

'I can believe it. Praying always gives me a dry throat, anyway.'

'Did you suffer much from the pestilence here?'

'It's eleven years ago now. '49 it hit us here. Suffer? Well, depends what you mean, I suppose. I've heard tales of how they went on in London, where they didn't even have time to give folks decent Christian burial, each in his own coffin, but had to pitch them all higgledy-piggledy into big pits. We weren't quite as bad as that here, of course. But when I was twenty years old, and that was in '48, the year before the first man died of the pestilence here, you had a job to hear mass properly of a Sunday. That was because there wasn't room. There were three masses on a Sunday, and St Mary's parish church has seats for three hundred and three people, never mind anybody standing at the back. It used to get full three times over; and if you were late you wouldn't get a seat. Now, since the pestilence came, there isn't call for more than two masses, and the church isn't above three-quarters full at either of those.'

'Good lord!'

'Ay. That was the way of it. I reckon it was like one of those plagues they had to put up with in Egypt. But '— the countryman shrugged his shoulders and winked—'when Paul cries Peter laughs, as they say.'

'Meaning?'

'When I was a nipper, good, strong, able-bodied men were three a penny in the Manor, and all up and down old England in all the other manors as well, I don't doubt—and they were treated as such. It's different now. Men are scarce; and what's scarce must be used a bit different from what's to spare.'

Young Geoffrey Chaucer was exhibiting his usual insatiable interest in human beings and all they had to tell him.

'You hold land in this Manor?' he asked.

'I do. John Wild is the name, and my father was John Wild before me. And his father, too, before him, if it comes to that. I hold thirty-four acres of good arable land off the Lord of Dalecombe Manor, in sixty-eight different strips all scattered about. I'm trying to get some of the strips together by swapping with other holders bit by bit. It's more sensible to get the holdings together a bit, especially now there aren't so many of us. But you can't get a lot of 'em to see it. And I hold four half-acre strips of pasture as well, and one of meadow; and I've common rights same as everybody else. And when they take me into Dalecombe churchyard my son will hold the same after me.'

'Amen to that,' Geoffrey said, laughing; and together he and the boy rode on into the yard of the Seven Stars Inn.

Here they met the miller, who had been sent on in advance to warn the landlord that the pilgrim party would want accommodation for the night.

The moment he spied them, the miller, a huge, full-bellied man, who must have weighed every bit of sixteen stone, rolled over towards them.

'It's God's mercy I did play harbinger and tell 'em we were all on the road,' he roared, his red beard wagging on his chin each time he spoke. 'There's to be a travelling show of some sort here tonight, and the place is seething like an eelpond already.'

'Have you fixed us up all right?'

The miller closed one lecherous eye in a self-satisfied wink.

'I have. But I don't believe anyone else in England could have done it. The mistress of the house reckoned she couldn't possibly cope with thirty people coming in, but I told her a handsome, well-set up woman like she is can always deal with anything; and she said if all the men in the party were to be like me——'

172

'Ay, ay, ay,' Geoffrey cut in. 'Spare us, spare us. We know, we know. You won her with the charm of your manner.'

'It's sober fact I did. And you can all be thankful for it.'

'Where are we lodged?' the boy asked, slipping off his horse and walking round to make sure whether his suspicion of a loose shoe on the near hind foot was justified or not.

'The Prioress, the two nuns, and the mistress from Bath are all withindoors. And if they aren't satisfied there they never will be, which, they being women, is only too likely, God knows.'

'And the rest?'

The miller jerked a hairy, spatulate thumb towards the far end of the yard.

'In the big barn. There's old hay there in plenty, and if a man can't sleep happy with old ale within and old hay without, then oaks never came from acorns, that's what I say.'

The boy had ascertained by now that his fears about a loose shoe were not very well-founded. True, the near hind shoe was not seated quite as firmly as it might be, but it was no immediate matter and it would serve a while yet.

He and Geoffrey made shift to get their horses comfortable before seeing to their own lodging.

The Seven Stars had blossomed lately from being a mere ale-house to an inn of some importance. Many men could remember when all it carried by way of advertisement was a holly bush stuck up on a pole; now the holly bush was gone and a painted sign, resplendent in blue and gold, had taken its place; the Seven Stars, Charles' Wain, hanging golden in a bright blue sky. The house itself, long and low, with two gables, faced the road, and behind it was the yard bounded by stables and out-buildings at the sides and the big barn at the back.

Only once or twice in a year could it have shown such a

scene of animation. By this time all the pilgrim party, even the stragglers, had ridden in and dismounted. The two handymen of the place, who normally looked after stabling the horses of any travellers, were quite unable to deal with this rush of work, and urgent demands had been sent into the town to see if any casual labourers could come and lend a hand.

All the horses were glad to have come to the end of the day and they were taking their turn, four at a time, drinking gratefully from a trough in one corner. It was one man's work to keep the trough replenished with water, and this was accomplished by a zany with long, light-coloured hair, who carried two buckets suspended from a yoke across his shoulders, making innumerable journeys with them from the well at the back of the house. In between times he stared with comically astonished eyes at all the bustle and confusion.

' Saints in the windows,' he kept saying to himself, ' saints in the windows. I've never seen such a deal of folk—and the Travelling Show as well, too.'

Actually the evidences of the Show had been a bit swamped for the time being by the arrival of the thirty pilgrims, but there was one sign of it that was unmistakably clear in the yard ; for there, in a corner of an inn in south-west England, fastened by a heavy iron chain to a stake driven well into the ground, and now curled up asleep on a piece of sacking, was a fair-sized, brown Himalayan bear. Its keeper sat by it, taking the opportunity to do some amateur cobbling to one of his shoes which had been too long on the road, and at a respectful distance stood a half-circle of lookers-on, children mostly, gazing in mute astonishment at the fabulous beast.

And the fabulous beast, who was only, after all, a poor bear, getting old now ; insufficiently fed ; cruelly used ; made to dance and hop and do all manner of degrading things ; perpetually chained and lugged about and shouted at and prodded with a sharp stick—this poor, fabulous beast, tired of walking ; tired of captivity ; tired of being stared at, lay curled up, taking no notice of anything or anybody. Perhaps he dreamed of another country and another time when he played in freedom, a small and happy cub by his mother's side.

The boy was in no particular hurry to get his nag, Starling, settled, and he took his time about watering and feeding the horse and tying it up in the stable. When that was done, he went round to the big barn and there staked out a place for himself for the night.

The barn was a grand building, newly put up, with great queen-posts and oaken roof-timbers towering overhead. The miller had been quite right about the hay ; there was any quantity of it there, and the men of the pilgrim party were not hesitating to pull the dry, clean stuff about in order to make themselves comfortable in it.

There was a good deal of laughing and chaffing ; and the miller was well to the fore in it all, cracking some of his innumerable jokes, especially at the expense of the one sailor among them, who came from Dartmouth, and who would persist each night in fixing up a home-made hammock he had brought with him. Not that the sailor minded being laughed at. Physically he was probably the toughest of them all, and he could afford to take any joking that came his way in good part. He just smiled and threw back a word here and there, and went on patiently fixing up his hammock.

The boy had very quickly got a place for himself, and he stood there quite a while in the dim barn, laughing at the fun going on and marvelling at the strange and rich and rewarding diversity of men.

After a while he strolled outside into the inn-yard again. One side of it now lay deep in shadow, for the April day was wearing to a close. There had been a fresh spattering of rain, but it had ceased almost as soon as it began and had only been sufficient to wet the cobbles.

The yard was now practically empty ; besides the boy himself, there was only a group in the far corner still staring at the bear, and in the centre of the yard the gaily dressed young Sir Thomas.

Through the open window of a bedroom the unmistakable voice of the old lady from Bath floated out in unmelodious complaint. It seemed that she had not been given the best bedroom in the place and that she thought she should have been given it. And she was letting the landlord know her mind on the subject in no uncertain manner. The landlord, whose thin, harassed voice could occasionally be heard like a frightened echo of hers, kept making excuses and saying something about ' the Prioress '.

' Holy ? Of course she's holy,' roared the irate lady of Bath. ' It's her business to be holy. And what's a holy woman want with the best bedroom, tell me that ? Where's her poverty and humility and all the rest of it ? I'm not . . .'

To the boy's disappointment, the lively discourse faded away there ; no doubt, he thought, because the landlord had retreated out of the room and the good lady of Bath had followed him, having no intention of letting him escape, with the result that her further remarks were not audible in the inn-yard.

He and young Sir Thomas smiled at one another in joint, but mute, appreciation of the dialogue they had overheard.

Then it happened.

A door in the back of the Seven Stars opened and somebody came out. She stood there and called : ' Taylor, Taylor.'

Those two words only ; but the boy knew in that instant that she had the most beautiful voice he had ever heard and that she herself was the loveliest creature he had ever seen. There was a gap in the yard buildings through which a ray of the now fast-setting sun came slanting in. It fell full on her ; and she stood in the soft yellow light, small and slim and upright.

176

The boy gazed at her entranced. He was young, and all the wonder of life lay ahead of him, and this was the first time that his heart had suddenly turned within him at the sight of a girl.

'Taylor' turned out to be the name of the regular ostler of the inn, who now came running forward with her mount from the small private stable.

The boy had to smile when he saw the dainty little grey palfrey, so well suited in its neatness, he couldn't help thinking, to the rider it was lucky enough to carry. The ostler held the horse whilst the girl mounted, which she did lightly and easily. While she was gathering her reins she said something about her mother coming on after, then with a smile to the ostler and a mere touch of her heel against the palfrey's flank she began to move off.

The boy had forgotten for the moment that young Sir Thomas existed; but that fashionable young gamecock was standing just beside him, and was gazing on the girl riding out of the inn-yard with the rapt expression of one who for the twentieth time had lost his heart to a vision.

It might all have ended there, with the girl on the grey palfrey riding out into the road and the two suddenly love-sick young swains staring blankly after her. It might have—but it didn't.

On her way round the inn-yard to gain the exit from it, the girl had to pass near the spot where the bear was tethered. Had she known it was there she would have been more careful; but the beast had been brought into the yard whilst she was in the inn itself, and was now in deep shadow.

The palfrey knew that something was there, in the dark shadow, by the disturbing and frightening scent which wafted up with sudden pungency to its nostrils; and it cocked its ears forward and showed the whites of its excitable eyes.

It had never experienced the smell of Bear before, and it

didn't like the smell of Bear. There were ancient, dark fears behind the smell, stretching far back into the morning of things, and they sent a shivering uneasiness through the palfrey's blood. The girl, being a good rider, was aware at once that something was the matter, and she began to take up her reins slightly.

'Stella, Stella,' she said gently ; but she was not quite in time. As they passed near it, the poor bear half-raised itself and moved—not, heaven knows, with any hostile intent, for all hostility had been knocked out of it long ago—but simply through sheer boredom.

But Stella, the five-year-old grey palfrey, knew nothing about the poor bear's boredom. All *she* knew was that a large hunk of darkness, with a very disturbing smell attached to it, had suddenly shifted in a most alarming manner under her very nose. And without the slightest hesitation or delay, and without pausing for one instant to find out whether or not there really was anything to be afraid of, she performed a remarkable combination of shy and rear, leaping smartly some three feet to the left and at the same time going straight
in the air on her hind legs.
up The sudden clash and clatter of her hooves on the cobbles frightened the bear, who let out a sort of snuffling grunt of alarmed inquiry, thus, of course, making things worse all round ; and the palfrey had no sooner come to earth from its first wild manœuvre than it was up again, more scared than ever.

The girl stuck on to the now madly plunging animal partly by luck, partly by virtue of the fact that she was a born rider ; one of those who know instinctively, a shadow of a second before it happens, what their mounts are going to do. But she only just managed to keep her seat, and was only too glad when assistance came to her from behind.

Both the boy and young Sir Thomas started forward, each

178

so intent on what he was doing that he scarcely realized the other was there. Between them, one on either side, they got the excited palfrey down to earth and persuaded it to see a bit of sense.

'It's the bear,' the boy cried. 'Get it away from the bear !'

'Of course it's the bear,' young Sir Thomas snapped. 'We all know that.'

All this talk of a bear was so much Greek to the girl, who thought privately that these two young men, whoever they were, must have taken leave of their senses ; but she was too much occupied with her pony at the moment to pay much attention to anything else.

'Stella, Stella,' she gentled with her lovely voice.

Reassured by a strong hand on either side of its bridle and by its mistress's comforting voice, the palfrey allowed itself to be led out to the roadway in front of the Seven Stars.

Here there were no deep shadows with blobs of darkness moving in them, nor was there that atavistic, frightening scent ; and after the irrational and stupid way of horses, the palfrey was quite prepared to believe that they had never really existed and to forget all about them. Everything was normal again and it couldn't think what all the fuss was about.

'By Saint Christopher, I thought you'd be off,' young Sir Thomas said.

The girl laughed. A pleasant, silvery sound.

'I thought I should, too. I've never known Stella behave like it. I can't imagine what frightened her so.'

'It was the bear, I fancy,' the boy said.

'Of course it was the bear.'

'The *bear* ?' the girl queried, puzzled.

'There's one in a corner of the inn-yard.'

'But how is there a bear in the yard of the Seven Stars ?'

'It's to be part of the Show tonight.'

'Are you coming to the Show?' young Sir Thomas asked eagerly.

The girl laughed again, the defensive laugh of one who for the moment is a bit bewildered by too many things happening at once around her.

'I—I hardly know,' she said. 'But first I must thank you—both. It was marvellous quick of you to catch my pony's head the way you did. I am in debt to both of you.' And as she said this she smiled, just as sweetly as any girl might ever smile—or so the two young men thought—and turned her head to them both, first to the left to where the boy looked up at her, and then quickly to young Sir Thomas on the other side.

'I don't suppose your nag has ever seen a bear before?' that young gentleman asked negligently, moving his arms so that his wide, embroidered sleeves showed to full advantage.

'In faith, no. Stella hasn't. Nor have I. There's never been a bear before in Dalecombe to my knowledge. Are you well acquainted with them, then?'

'When I was in Picardy with the cavalry we used to see them sometimes in the streets of the towns, being led about and dancing.'

'Picardy?' The girl gazed in frank admiration at the young gentleman of fashion who had been to Picardy; then suddenly she turned her head and smiled at the other young gentleman who had come to her rescue; a smile that seemed to be meant for him and him alone.

'And you, sir?' she inquired roguishly. 'Have you, too, been to Picardy and seen bears there?'

The boy hadn't. He wished he had. He wished he could say that he had been to Picardy, Flanders, Artois, to Algiers and Alexandria, to any of the places in Christendom whose names rang like trumpets of adventure. Anything to hold

180

her attention, and to vie with the jaunty young Sir Thomas on the other side. But the best he could manage was:

'I once saw a man in Bristol with two small monkeys—marmosets, I think he called them——'

'Two small monkeys in Bristol!' young Sir Thomas thought it was the funniest thing he had heard for a long time, and laughed loud accordingly. 'That's brave sport, I must say.'

The boy flushed a little and the girl on Stella said quickly:

'I've never seen two small monkeys; or been to Bristol, for that matter. You are both men of travel, I can see.'

'You should ride with your leathers longer,' young Sir Thomas said. 'You'd sit your horse better.'

The girl had not the slightest intention of lengthening her stirrup leathers. Stella was her mount and nobody else's, and she knew exactly how to sit and handle the pony. So she answered impishly:

'I'm sure if you've been in the cavalry you know all about riding, but'—swivelling round to the boy and putting the question to him—'what do *you* think?'

'I think everybody should ride the way they find best for themselves,' he replied sturdily, 'and not listen to others.'

Young Sir Thomas ignored this and, running his hand familiarly over the palfrey's dappled neck, asked:

'Do you live in Dalecombe, then?'

The girl raised the short crop she carried to make a vague point with it.

'Up at the Manor.'

'Your father is Lord of the Manor, perhaps?'

'He is.'

'My father is Sir Thomas Treyhearne the Knight.'

'And *my* father is a wine merchant of the City of London.' Young Geoffrey Chaucer had come from out of the inn-yard just in time to add his irrepressible bit to the conversation.

It made the girl throw back her head and laugh merrily.

'I'm not used to such high company,' she said. 'We are quiet people here in Dalecombe.'

'But you are coming to see the Show here tonight?' young Sir Thomas asked eagerly, ignoring Geoffrey's light-hearted interruption.

She shrugged her shoulders. 'How can I?'

'But why not? You would not want for a squire.'

Again the girl let her silver laughter ripple out. She spread her hands, for there were now three young men about her.

'So much I see,' she said.

'I mean I would act as your squire gladly,' young Sir Thomas amended hastily.

'But——'

'And there will be much to see: tumblers, jugglers, the bear——'

'You are very persuasive, young sir knight.'

'And you are ve——'

It was the perfect opportunity for a pretty compliment and clearly young Sir Thomas intended to seize it.

'Curse all these smooth-tongued, fashionable young fops,' the boy thought, listening in great annoyance. 'They get away with it every time, somehow.'

But this time, at least, young Sir Thomas didn't get away with his intended compliment, for he was interrupted and cut short by a stentorian voice from the front door of the inn demanding:

'Where's my horse?'

And this was followed almost immediately by a second surprised inquiry in the same commanding tones.

'Miss Alison, what are you doing here? I told you to be riding on. You should be nigh home by now.'

There could be no missing or mistaking the authority of

the tones in which these two remarks were not so much uttered as shouted. Anyone who hadn't seen that they issued from a tall, impressive-looking woman would have thought that it was a man calling out, and all three young men had the sense to keep quiet.

'I was starting out home,' the girl began to explain, 'but Stella got frightened by a bear——'

'A *bear*!' It almost sounded as though the bear itself were growling. 'Don't try to be funny, child. I see no bear delaying you; I see three young gentlemen in attendance on you.'

'Will you please allow me to present them to you, Mother, for two of them helped to quieten Stella when she reared.'

'If that nag of yours is going to start to rear you can get rid of her, child. I've no use for a rearing horse or a railing hussy.'

'Stella's perfectly well behaved as a rule, Mother.'

'Ah, like you, my dear, I expect. But there seem to be moments when the rule gets broken.'

'And these are the three gentlemen I should like to present to you. Sir Thomas Treyhearne, my mother, Mistress Forester.'

Young Sir Thomas performed mightily gallant with his flourish and bow, as he had seen them done at King Edward's court at Westminster. It even crossed his mind that he might try kissing the lady's hand, but after a second look at her he decided not to.

The girl Alison turned quickly to the boy on her other side and snared him for a moment in her silver smile.

'I'm so sorry,' she said, 'I don't know your name——'

He gave it to her and she repeated it to her mother.

The boy inclined his head and mumbled something, wishing to heaven he didn't feel so stiff and awkward about it.

Young Geoffrey Chaucer, who was never at a loss in any

184

company, moved forward and said easily : ' And my name is Geoffrey Chaucer, son of John Chaucer of London.'

Whilst this had been going on, Taylor had made a second appearance, this time leading a tall, powerful-looking black horse, that looked as though it knew exactly how it was expected to behave and had much too much sense to try any tricks.

Mistress Forester mounted it inelegantly but with a vast amount of assurance ; and when she was securely and comfortably seated she said :

' I make no doubt you three young gentlemen have seen my daughter before somewhere, for you seem to be remarkably well acquainted all of a sudden.'

' I had hopes, madam,' said young Sir Thomas, coming forward gallantly, ' of seeing her again soon.'

' Had you now, sir ? '

Undeterred by her tone, young Sir Thomas courageously stuck his ground ; and, to the rather unwilling admiration of the boy, continued :

' I thought, madam, that perhaps, this evening, your daughter might care to see the spectacle, such as it is, that will be presented here.'

' You thought wrong, sir.'

The formidable Mistress Forester gathered her reins, gave her black horse a good, hard, no-nonsense kick in the ribs, and, looking straight ahead of her, set off for the Manor.

The little group of three men, with Taylor the ostler a few paces behind, stood in front of the Seven Stars watching mother and daughter, the tall bony black and the dainty grey palfrey, ride off.

The horses had not gone twenty paces when Alison turned her head quickly and smiled. Not only did she smile, but she raised one small, gloved hand and sketched a fascinating little gesture of a farewell salute with it. It would have taken

Solomon himself to say which of the three young men that smile and that wave of her small hand were meant for. But youth knows better than Solomon, and the moment the two riders were out of earshot and talk was safe, young Sir Thomas burst out triumphantly :

'Did you see her smile and wave at me ?'

'I saw her smile and wave,' Geoffrey said.

'At who else but me, then ?'

'I thought it was at our friend here.'

'Oh come—I was the one talking to her all the time, and she was looking straight at me.'

'Or at the good Taylor behind us,' Geoffrey added solemnly.

'Ah——'

In the background Taylor laughed. 'Have your fun, young gentlemen,' he croaked raspily. 'Why not ? If the young cock won't crow, what shall ? That's what I say. Miss Alison's as proper a young lady as ever sat at her spinning-wheel. But don't forget'—he laughed throatily—'him as steals the chick may get a peck from the hen.'

With which piece of advice he stumped off on his thin legs back to his buckets, his straw, and his sweetly-sour smelling stables.

Young Sir Thomas paid no attention to him. His fancies were still running furiously elsewhere.

'If the old dragon hadn't come out at that moment,' he said, 'she would have said " yes " to coming here tonight.'

'But whom would she have said it to ?' Geoffrey teased him.

'I do not think she would have looked to the Vintners of the City of London for her escort,' young Sir Thomas said rudely.

For a moment Geoffrey Chaucer flushed ; but he was wise beyond his years ; he had learned already that it takes

186

all sorts to make a world, and that a quarrel is a tedious matter.

'Who knows what a lady's choice might be?' he said easily; and he and the boy walked back together across the inn-yard to the barn.

The first hubbub of settling down had died away now and most of the pilgrims were out, either in the Seven Stars itself, washing the dust of travel out of their throats, or else exploring the small town of Dalecombe to see what there was of it. But a few were left in the barn. One of them was the carpenter, an honest fellow from Exeter, who was working on the roof of the nave which was slowly being added to the cathedral there.

It was the roof of the barn that was catching his attention now; and certainly in the dim light above it showed up with massive impressiveness.

'There's work for you,' he said to Geoffrey and the boy as they came in through the huge doorway. 'Look at those timbers. All sawed in the pit and seasoned. English oak as sweet as ever came out of English woodlands. That roof will stand these five hundred years and more.'

The boy tried to imagine what the world would look like in five hundred years' time, but gave it up with a laugh.

'Now in Exeter,' the carpenter was saying, 'it's neater work in a way, closer as you may say, more to gauge and rule. But it's no better; that I must admit. A man as loves timber, loves timber and uses it right all the world over. Free masons they talk about; but free carpenters, I say. There's no craft like it. Wasn't Christ Himself a carpenter and worked at the bench the best part of thirty years?'

The boy would cheerfully have listened to much of this man's talk, which was as much thinking aloud as actual conversation; but Geoffrey was nudging him in the ribs.

'Here's something more to the point than carpentry,' he whispered.

'But this is interesting, Geoffrey.'

'I've a notion this might be, too.'

Geoffrey took him by the arm and steered him to where, a dozen yards away, one man sat on a bale of hay writing, and another stood by his side. The seated man they both recognized as the studious scholar from Oxford, who looked even thinner and more scarecrow-like dismounted than he had done on his poor nag.

The man talking to him was the Dartmouth sailor, who stood with hairy arms akimbo, and a comically puzzled look on his berry-brown face.

The boy was surprised at this unlikely conjunction.

'What do these two make together?' he said.

'Clerk's work, I guess,' Geoffrey replied with a laugh, 'for if it's true, as the tinkers and pedlars say, that a sailor has a wife in every port—why, there must be plenty of letter writing to do.'

'I'd sooner him than me, for if there's one thing I can't abide to do it's to write letters.'

'So?' Geoffrey said. 'I don't mind it so much myself. My pen's no enemy to me. If I sit at desk and draw the paper in front of me the words come; but—I wonder what sort of hand this learned man from Oxford writes?'

'Why, Geoffrey?'

A mischievous twinkle danced for a moment in young Chaucer's lively dark eyes.

'Who knows?' he said. 'Who knows? There's always sport to be had in the world if you look for it hard enough, say I. And what does the scripture say about pride going before a fall?'

'Now you *are* babbling.'

'Maybe, maybe. Let's draw near and see.'

Together they moved forward a few paces, just in time
to hear the scholar's precise voice saying, as he prepared to
write the words :

'*Ergo*, it follows. . . .'

'Ay, ay, ay. No doubt it does, Master Scholar,' the
bemused sailor broke in. '*Ergo* this and *propter* that, and
abracadabra and all the rest of it.'

'Not *abracadabra*,' the scholar corrected gently. 'That's
something I've no use for. *Barbara* perhaps, one of the figures
of the syllogism.'

'But it isn't syllogisms I want, Master Scholar ; and it
isn't syllogisms my Martha wants back in Dartmouth. You
know how the tavern jokes go——'

'I'm afraid I'm not very well versed in the current talk
of the taverns.'

'No, no. Of course not. But about us sailors, I mean.
We're supposed to have a different wife at every port we look
in at. By Saint Paul's shipwreck, if I had a wife at every
port of call I make I'd be as bad as the heathen king in Barbary,
or wherever it is. And I don't want 'em. All I want is my
Martha living in Anchor Cottage on the Hard at Dartmouth.
That's all I want you to tell her, Master Scholar, no *ergos* or
quids or *quods* or any of your learned stuff. Just that I hope
she's as fit as I am, and here we are at Dalecombe on the way,
and there's a bear in the yard, and I'll pray for her when I
get to St Thomas's shrine, and to be sure to keep the pig
fed as I told her, and I haven't seen a woman yet I'd look at
twice if she was about, and I don't expect to either, and she
has my heart her captive as well she knows, and so much love
your faithful husband Francis. Oh—and not to forget the
beans.'

'The beans ?'

'Ay. The second sowing of broad beans should be done
this month whilst the moon waxes.'

'That's a thing I haven't learnt at Queen's College,' the scholar said. 'And all knowledge is good.'

He bent himself over the task of finishing the Epistle to Martha to the satisfaction of the sailor, who had somehow discovered that a train of pack-horses carrying cloth was stabling that night at the other, smaller inn in Dalecombe, and would be setting off for the west country in the morning.

When the letter was finished the scholar from Queen's College read it through.

'. . . no *ergos* or *quods* or *quidlibets*,' he said, smiling. 'How does that suit you?'

The simple sailor was vastly pleased.

'Nay, that's a masterpiece. That's as I meant it. Just what I wanted to say. What a thing to be able to write!' he cried, turning to the other two standing by.

'Ay,' Geoffrey Chaucer echoed dreamily. 'What a thing to be able to write, to be sure!'

'And payment?' the sailor asked, putting his hand to his wallet. 'What account do I owe you?'

'Nothing,' the Oxford man answered quickly.

'Nothing? How's that?'

'I can prove that I owe you something, Master Sailor,' the scholar told him.

'Nay, if you can prove that, you can *ergo* and all the rest of it to some purpose, I'll allow.'

'Listen then: let it run thus: every man who gives another the opportunity of acquiring merit places that other in his debt. Shall we take that as our Major Premise; a Universal Affirmative; an A?'

The sailor, a bit bewildered, nodded.

'And to proceed: by giving me the chance to do a good deed in this matter of sending back word from an honest husband to a loving wife, you are one who has given to another, *videlicit* me, the opportunity of acquiring merit.'

' Lord save us.'

' Suppose that to be our Minor Premise ; a Particular Affirmative ; an I.'

' Is this what goes on at Queen's College, Oxford ? ' the sailor asked.

' All the time, my friend. All truth in the world must yield to the force of logic. So, to complete our own syllogism, let us draw the Conclusion, which now must clearly be another Particular Affirmative, another I, giving us the figure *darii*—you know the jingle :

' *Barbara, celarent, darii, ferio, baralipton prioris.*'

' St Elmo's fire ! ' the sailor exclaimed. ' What does all that mean ? '

' It means that our Conclusion is, and you cannot possibly deny it, that it is now firmly and clearly established that you are a person who has put me in your debt, and since a debtor is one who owes something to another, *ergo* I owe you something. *Quod erat demonstrandum.*'

The sailor put the folded and addressed letter away carefully in his wallet.

' I'll be going to find the master of the pack-horse train and a pot of ale,' he said solemnly. ' I'm mightily obliged to you, Master Scholar, but if I stay listening to you another minute you'll have my head as addled as a month-old egg.'

As the honest sailor went out, Geoffrey laughed.

' You do a kind act neatly, sir,' he said. ' I could wish I were up at Oxenford with you.'

' You were not of the University ? '

' No. Not I. I got what schooling I could in St Paul's Almonry, London, and then went as page into a great house.'

' Whose ? '

' Her Grace of Clarence—well, at that time she was Countess of Ulster.'

191

'The world of fashion.'

'But not of logic.'

'Logic is not very fattening.'

'Nay, if you do a man a service and then prove yourself in debt to him you are not likely to get fat.'

'True, true. But who could take a fee for helping a simple man to send his love to his wife?'

'A number that I know of,' Geoffrey said dryly. 'But tell me, if we chop logic for fun, is laughter a good or a bad thing?'

'Primarily and *simpliciter* good. And demonstrably so from the scriptures. Does not the text go: *there was laughter in Paradise before Evil came?*'

'I'm not your man for texts,' Geoffrey said. 'I'll warrant there's a text to prove anything you've a mind to. But I've always been one for a bit of fun.'

'Fun?' the scholar echoed, looking, it must be confessed, like a man who has not seen overmuch of that commodity in his life.

'Not to put too fine a point on it, a practical joke. I want a letter written.'

'I can write a letter, true.'

'We have just seen how well you can do so.'

The Oxford man smiled and looked up at Geoffrey. 'But you can surely write, too?' he said. 'I've a notion that a pen and you are no strangers to one another.'

'I can write,' Geoffrey agreed, 'but this particular letter is one in which I don't want my own handwriting to appear. When we started only two days ago the old Knight asked me to write out for him a list of all in our company, each person's name, and who they were, and where from—in order, as the good old chap said, that he might know his adopted family. Not much sooner said than done. Nothing in that. But the point is this: what the old Knight saw, 'tis almost certain the young Sir Thomas his son will also have looked at. That was only yesterday, and it's more than likely that the young gamecock, seeing my hand again, would remember and recognize it.'

'And you don't want young Sir Thomas to do that?'

Geoffrey laughed and shook his head. 'All would be spoilt,' he said.

The Oxford scholar considered a moment, biting the end of his quill pen.

'Is there harm for anybody in this jape?' he asked at length.

'No harm at all, that I promise you. Fun only. And maybe a bit of good done into the bargain.'

'The young man struts a trifle, assuredly.'

'Then listen . . .' Geoffrey said, and outlined his scheme.

When he had finished the scholar laughed and pulled inkhorn and paper before him again.

'If you can make your hand look like a girl's, so much the better,' Geoffrey told him. 'You know how a lady writes.'

'In faith I don't,' the Oxford man said, maybe a little sadly. 'It's few enough letters I get from anyone, and none ever from a lady. It grows mighty dark in here.'

'The light's going,' Geoffrey said, 'it's well past six o'clock and cloudy.'

'And what do you wish to say, madam, to this ardent young swain of yours?'

'Let's see now—how should I, being a girl and lovely, and smitten of a sudden passion for a young man I have just met for the first time, how should I set about telling him I want to see him again soon—shall we start so?'

'No, not that way.'

'Why not thus and thus?'

'Or thus and thus?'

' Oh brave, brave.'

' Exactly it, exactly.'

So between the three of them, and with a deal of laughter, the note was written, the bait prepared.

' Read it,' Geoffrey said, when the last flourish was done and dry ; and the man from Oxford, who, for a while, had forgotten Aristotle and his philosophy, held up the sheet to catch the light from the big doorway of the barn.

> *The Manor House,*
> *Tuesday even.*
>
> *You must not be surprised that my mother cut short our talk this afternoon, after you had so bravely and quickly come to my help. She is of the old school, and if she seemed to show you rudeness I would fain make amends. I shall ride towards the town to see the spectacle tonight, and if you come out to meet me I know I shall have a true knight and a brave for company and protection. Ride out at eight o'clock on the road towards the Manor and we shall meet in the way. I send this by the hand of a countryman and must end quickly or Madame will ask to know what I am doing. My heart is impatient for the evening.*
>
> *Alison.*

' What did the sailor say about his letter—a masterpiece he called it, didn't he ? ' Geoffrey cried. ' Nay, this *is* a masterpiece. The three of us should turn scribe and wax fat, writing love-letters for the town. This lure will draw the young falcon, no fear.'

' And the super-scripture ? '

' To Young Sir Thomas Treyhearne at the sign of the Seven Stars ; write flourishes, man, write flourishes ; young ladies are always taught to put plenty of flourishes. And add at the bottom, in the corner here, " by hand ". So. Good, good.'

'And how do we show the lure to the hawk?' the boy inquired.

'Come with me,' Geoffrey said, leading the way out of the barn. 'We need an Ambassador now; and I've a notion where we can find one.'

They found him in the tap-room at the back of the inn, sitting there gravely and soberly among his peers, listening to the small talk of the town and to the old man telling stories of the brave days of his youth from the chimney corner. His pot stood all but empty before him.

They slid down on to the seat, one on either side of him.

'John Wild,' Geoffrey said, 'your pot's empty.'

'Likely to be,' the countryman answered, 'with beer at a penny the pint. What's England coming to if a man can't have his skinful of beer?'

Geoffrey made a sign to the potman and paid for the necessary replenishment. Then out of his wallet he drew four separate pennies and placed them on the massive oak board of the table; an operation which John Wild watched with interest and curiosity.

'That's a fee,' Geoffrey told him. 'That's wages. That's to be earned.'

'How? Dyking, hedging, delving, ploughing, thatching, poaching, coney-catching, wrestling, running? I'm your man for any of these.'

'I wouldn't doubt you. Nothing of that.'

'You want one of your horses shod or drenched? Or maybe there's a bit of harness wants mending?'

'Maybe there is. Let it be. If we go to pray to St Thomas, St Thomas must look after us on the way, say I. All you need do is to carry this letter round to the front door of the Seven Stars here and ask boldly for young Sir Thomas Treyhearne, who, as befits their quality, is sitting drinking with his respected father in the private parlour.'

'That's not hard work.'

'And you'll not forget, if asked, who gave you the letter?'

'Once I'm told I'll not forget. A fee gives me a good memory. Who was it?'

'A young lady, as you came walking close by the Manor House, asked you to carry it here.'

'Did she now?'

'Somewhat mysteriously.'

'I'll warrant. Is this a game, young sirs, a jape?'

'That's it.'

'No harm to anyone?'

'None. Only some laughs and maybe a feather or two moulted from a peacock's tail.'

John Wild drained his newly filled pot in two mighty draughts, pocketed his fee, and stood up. 'I've not carried a letter before,' he said. 'But why not? The way the world is, the old dog must learn new tricks in order to thrive, that's how I see things.' He winked, and made his way over the sawdust-strewn floor to the door.

'And now?' the boy asked. 'What next?'

'In the household of that noble but rather irritable lady, the Countess of Ulster,' Geoffrey said, as though he were reading out the first chapter of a romance, 'it was always the fashion to present plays four or even six times a year, at Christmas and other big feasts. When there was a lady's part to be enacted no one could do it better than the young page newly joined to the great establishment; one Master Geoffrey Chaucer, son of a wine merchant in the City of London.'

The boy laughed. 'What fun!'

'Yes. I was always the girl; and, believe me, dressed up a bit with some old things and oddments from one of the ladies' wardrobes I made such a fetching Miss as set all the young gallants talking.'

'But, Geoffrey——'

'How now?'

'One thing we lack. The wardrobe——'

'Not entirely,' Geoffrey answered, getting up. 'At least, I hope not. The fat mistress of Bath carries packages enough. She's got something we can borrow with advantage, I'll warrant.'

'But will she lend it?'

Geoffrey winked one worldly eye.

'She's a woman,' he said. 'None more so. And there's engines of war and devices to lay siege to a woman's heart.'

He took a look outside and said : 'It's all but dark now and the light will be quite gone soon. There'll be a moon ; but the sky looks cloudy enough to hide it. It must be every bit of half-past six already, and we ought to leave in an hour. You see to the horses and I'll go campaigning against the formidable City of Bath!'

Outside, the inn-yard, which had seethed with activity on the arrival of the pilgrim train, but had lapsed into a period of comparative quiet again after all that fuss had settled down, was now beginning to be alive once more.

Along one side three booths had already been set up, and a fourth was being erected. A noisy argument was in progress as to whether there was room for this fourth and last stall, the three stall-holders already in possession loudly maintaining that there was not ; the would-be fourth stall-holder even more loudly insisting that there was.

And the person who wished to set up the fourth booth was nobody to be put lightly aside. She was none other than the Fat Woman from Taunton, who had toured all the West of England and was making her way slowly towards London.

The boy was fascinated and repelled by her. She was short and dark, and had a mole on one cheek with three long black hairs straggling from it. She was enormously, repulsively, fat, with short, stumpy legs whose folds of flesh seemed to flow over the tops of her shoes. A pole had been set up by one stall-holder with a horn lantern hanging from it, and in the yellow candlelight thrown out by this her pasty face fairly glistened with perspiration.

By her side, watching with beady eyes the outcome of her wordy battle, was the little hunchback dwarf who, once she got established, would act as attendant, door-keeper, money-taker, and general manager.

'Live and let live,' she was demanding in a husky voice. 'Where's Christian charity, where's justice?'

'Nay, Mother, I haven't got them in my stall,' the next-door man said. 'I deal in gingerbread, nothing else.'

'And won't everyone who sees the Fat Woman want to eat a gingerbread after?' she demanded.

'Want a strong draught, more like,' said somebody from the dark background; and in the general laugh that followed the dispute somehow got washed away; and at a nod from his fat mistress the hunchback began to set up the bit of a tent.

Beyond the gingerbread stall was one occupied by Doctor Phalerous, who was able, as a large banner displayed in front assured anyone able to read, to determine instantly the natural humour of any man, whether hot, cold, dry, or moist, and who could supply pills guaranteed to cure an excess of any one of these qualities. He was also an expert in Love Potions and Charms of all sorts, and had an Infallible Cure for Warts and Carbuncles.

Beyond him was a cheap-jack stall set up by a thin, mournful-looking Jew, who had been born and brought up in the Jewry at Lincoln, and who, as a boy, had seen dark and dreadful things done to his tribe in the narrow alleys between the overhanging houses of that city.

Eli, as he was called, had somehow escaped these excesses and had come to terms with the Christians among whom he lived; and now he spent a nomad life going from fair to

fair, from market-place to market-place, scrupulously careful always to pay the fee demanded and to avoid any sort of quarrel. When talk grew loud and excited, and men waxed red in the face and shouted at one another and shook fists, Eli, the tall, thin, grave-faced Jew, stood quietly on one side and watched the folly of the warring world with sad, sardonic eyes. And as soon as the shouting and swearing was over he fell instantly to trade again, with the same sardonic and steady eyes watching the Christians as they came jostling one another, fingering his linens and cambrics, rummaging among his second-hand clothes, over-eager to buy, ignorant how to bargain.

The other stalls each had two horn lanterns hanging up, but his one only.

On the opposite side of the yard, each forming their own little encampment, were the jugglers, the wrestlers, the tumblers, and the man who walked on stilts. Each had something in the way of gear to be got ready, or clothes to be looked to ; and as the boy walked slowly round the yard, stopping every few yards to eavesdrop, each little group had talk to listen to. The eternal talk of Show People. The talk of the road. Where last they had set up their stand ; where next they hoped to do so. Of how business was or wasn't. Of what acquaintances had been seen, or heard of lately ; of what friends had dropped out or died. Of the iniquity of market and fair dues rigorously exacted by this lord or that ; of the agreeable laxity, but this was rare, to be found some-where else. Of the ale-houses and inns of England they talked, so that there seemed (to the boy's listening ears) to be nothing on the roads but White Lions, Green Men, Stars of various numbers, Salutations, Nags' Heads, Horses of different colours, and Saints of every sort.

The far corner was still occupied by the bear, now in a wooden cage covered over with sacking.

'He doesn't like the lights,' his master explained surlily to the boy. 'Can't abide them. They make 'im wild.'

'He doesn't look very wild to me.'

The man exhibited a short, thick stake sharpened at one end to a brutal point.

'If 'e gets wild 'e gets *this*,' he said, 'that's the way to keep the devils right.'

Whilst all these preparations were going on, the public were denied entrance to the yard. A rope was drawn across the entrance and Taylor the ostler, reinforced by local help, kept all and sundry out.

The arrangement was that the Fat Woman, the gingerbread vendor, and all the rest of them paid so much to mine host of the Seven Stars for the privilege of exhibiting or performing in his yard ; and in turn mine host had to make what he might by charging a penny, or less, for admittance to outsiders, and by taking up a collection among the people resident at the inn. Not that he minded a great deal about either the price of admission or the collection, for a spectacle like this meant business in the parlour and the tap-room ; such business as would not be equalled more than two or three times in the year.

Watching all this, listening to it, *feeling* it as part of the colour and excitement of being alive, kept the boy an entranced observer, but he forced himself away from it all to see that his own horse and Geoffrey's were ready for use when they should be wanted. He felt sorry to ask the animals to turn out again now that they were watered and fed, but at least he knew that it would not be for any very arduous task.

When he came away from the stables, satisfied that all was ready, he saw young Sir Thomas sauntering towards them with a very well-satisfied air, and the sight amused him.

Someone was singing in the tap-room of the Seven Stars now, a man, in a rough voice, but not unmelodiously ; and after every verse the whole company with him would crash out into the chorus.

Now the boy did indeed stand entranced by the scene as the horn lanterns, swinging in the slight breeze, threw monstrous moving shadows across the many-peopled yard, and the singing floated out from the inn on the darkness of the April night. They were singing an old song which each generation had learnt from their fathers before them, forgetting a few of the words, altering others, misunderstanding some ; but essentially retaining the same thing. A song about old and ancient things in England, about the days of the Romans, and then about the long darkness that followed when the legions went, and about the iron rule of Duke William.

The boy was listening to it, not knowing all that it was about, but at least aware that it was something more than just a roaring good drinking-tune, when a girl's voice spoke low at his side.

He turned quickly, a little startled, and there in the dark was a feminine figure wrapped up against the night.

The low whisper came again and the boy said : ' I'm sorry. I didn't hear what you said.'

' How's this for the best the old lady of Bath could do for me ? ' Geoffrey repeated, using his own voice.

' Good lord ! You ! '

Geoffrey laughed softly. ' It will pass, don't you think ? ' he asked. ' In the darkness, at a few respectful feet away ? '

' It's wonderful.'

' I had but to tell Madame Bath that I was engaged in an amorous intrigue, and she ransacked her wardrobe for me. I had also to stop her coming herself to see the sport.'

' Heaven forbid.'

' Are the horses ready ? '

' Ready ; but not very willing, I fear, poor nags. Not

that we shall take them far. And young Sir Thomas has gone to get his.'

'Has he? Then we should be starting. Come on.'

Their setting out caused no comment, for Dalecombe, especially immediately round the Seven Stars, was full of strangers that evening, and if a young lady chose to ride forth with a gentleman for escort, what of it?

They dared not do more than walk, for Geoffrey, to suit his part, had to ride side-saddle, and since he had no proper side-saddle, it was no easy task to stick on.

'The devil take this for a game,' he complained. 'It's a mercy we haven't far to go.'

'How far?'

'The Manor House isn't more than a mile and a half away. I learnt it all from a serving wench in the Stars. This road takes us straight to it if we keep right at the fork. I wouldn't ride five miles like this for a fortune. I'd either die of cramp in the leg or be on my backside on the road. Quintal doesn't think much of it, either.'

Quintal was the name of Geoffrey's ungainly, mustard-coloured horse, which in any case strongly objected to turning out again when the proper day's work was obviously over, and in addition couldn't imagine why its rider had got his weight all wrong on top of it, and wasn't sitting properly. With the foolish apprehensiveness that possesses all horses to a greater or lesser degree, it had already come to the conclusion that something must be the matter, and was moving its ears backwards and forwards ready to magnify any innocent sound into something formidable and frightening.

The stir and bustle around the Seven Stars was soon left behind, and where Dalecombe straggled away in its last few houses everything was dark and quiet.

There was no difficulty in following the way, for it lay between two high banks, and when at last these ran down to nothing, meeting the general level of the land on either hand, the road forked, offering on the left a mere deep-rutted track into the fields, and on the right the obvious continuation of the way to the Manor.

Perhaps a couple of hundred yards from this fork there was a small spinney of beech-trees which lined the road on either side.

'The very spot,' Geoffrey said; for the clouds were clearing unexpectedly and the moonlight was beginning to be effective. 'The very spot, here, in the shadows. And thank heaven I've got here safely. I don't believe I could have done another quarter-mile in this trussed cockerel position.'

Under the tall, straight beeches the moonlight came through only in patches and there were pools of deep black shadow.

They had hardly drawn rein before the boy cocked his head.

'There's a horse coming,' he said. 'Trotting.'

'You've sharp ears,' Geoffrey complimented him in a whisper. 'Do you go forward a little, behind those three trees there. They'll hide you. I'll wait here in this bit of shadow.'

'I hope he doesn't recognize your nag.'

'Poor old Quintal's ugly enough. But I'll keep him in the dark. And I don't think our young gallant's eyes will be noticing horse-flesh much tonight. At least I'll do my best to divert him.' Here he dropped his voice into the half-whisper, half-girlish giggling tone which for a moment had completely misled the boy in the inn-yard: '*I was hoping, sir, for an escort into the town, and a true knight and a brave one for company and protection.*'

The boy struck his saddle pommel in delight. 'Monstrously good,' he cried.

'Quiet, quiet. I can hear him coming now. Away you go out of sight, and we'll see what sport the wine merchant's son has with the gentleman.'

Young Sir Thomas's chestnut with the three white socks didn't care about turning out again any more than the other horses had done. It was consequently in a bad temper and anxious only to get the job, whatever it might be, finished and return to its stall. It took a poor view, therefore, of being reined to a halt when the outlines of another horse and its rider showed dimly in the dark shadows.

Young Sir Thomas took no poor view of it, however. His blood ran young and hot, and Dalecombe had seemed at first to offer but poor opportunity for amusement. Now, totally unexpectedly, this adventure, which was very much to his liking, had fallen into his lap. The pretty girl coming out of the inn . . . the trouble with her horse . . . his ready help (the ready help of others, too ; but he chose to forget that) . . . her provocative leave-taking of him under the very eyes of her dragon-mother . . . then, when all seemed inevitably lost and over, the countryman with the letter. . . .

Oh yes, indeed, this was just the sort of gallant adventure that the young man loved and which he expected to befall him as a matter of right. It just showed, he thought, what came of wearing one of the now fashionable embroidered cottes with the wide sleeves, and of having, even if he did say it himself, as shapely a leg as was ever shown at court.

'Stand, Pagan, you devil,' he growled, trying to make the impatient chestnut see sense, and at the same time sweeping off his hat in a very impressive gesture.

'Mistress Forester,' he said, 'it was wonderfully good of you to send me that letter.'

He was disappointed not to see her face straightway, but on the whole he was not surprised if she chose to be muffled up almost to her eyes. It must clearly be without her mother's knowledge that she was keeping this tryst, and she would be scared.

'She'll thaw out,' young Sir Thomas promised himself. 'I'll see to that.'

He could hardly catch her whispered reply.

'Come, don't be scared,' he said. 'My lady, your mother, is safely back in the Manor, I'll warrant, and doesn't suspect a thing.'

The muffled head nodded.

'You could perhaps unveil a little,' young Sir Thomas suggested. ''Tis a pity to hide up a beautiful face.'

'Oh, sir,' came the whispered reply.

'Nay, but I mean it. I never thought in Dalecombe to see such a lovely girl.'

'Nor I such a true, brave knight.'

'Well, well, that's as maybe,' young Sir Thomas said, mightily pleased. 'Shall we not be riding back into the town to see the fun at the inn?'

He found it difficult to catch the reply; it was whispered so low; something encouraging, however, about '. . . like nothing better.'

'Come,' he said, speaking out loud and clear, 'there's no one to overhear us here. Let's talk out and enjoy ourselves.'

When the other horse began to move forward from the shadows into the moonlight it caught his eye at once. He had a thought for a moment that it seemed vaguely familiar.

'You ride a different horse, Mistress Forester,' he said, 'from that skittish palfrey of yours.'

The boy was safely hidden hardly a dozen yards away; his ears were stretched to catch every syllable of this remarkable conversation, and he had serious fears that he might strain something within him by the effort to hold back his laughter. It seemed to him that Geoffrey might find the next few moments distinctly trying, particularly if the observant young

Sir Thomas pursued the matter of the horse ; but at that moment something happened.

A large white thing, eerie in the moonlight and astonishing in the suddenness of its appearance, came *whoosh* down the clearing between the trees, almost brushing his face with its wings. It startled them all ; but it did more than startle Quintal. Quintal had mistrusted the whole business from the start, and he was unused to owls, anyway. He went straight up in the air in indignation and alarm ; and Geoffrey, who was only sitting there by luck and a trick of balance, slithered down on the ground—*bump*.

Perhaps you may get away with the pretence of being a young lady whilst sitting motionless, muffled up and in the shadows ; but it is a very different matter when you are spread-eagled on the ground, your two legs waving in the air, out in the full moonlight.

' What the devil—' young Sir Thomas began in bewilderment ; and then the laughter started.

The boy began it from his hiding-place behind the trees. You can bottle up laughter within yourself for so long ; but only for so long ; then something bursts. Laughter came out from him in great shrieks and guffaws, all the louder now for having been held back for so long.

And when Geoffrey got over the immediate shock of hitting the ground well and truly with the base of his spine and heard that laughter coming from behind him in the trees, he realized that the ludicrous game was up and joined in with all his heart and soul.

Presently he had struggled to his feet and was leaning against his horse, which was patiently nibbling at some sparse tufts of grass, whilst the boy had moved forward into the clearing and was standing by his mount ; and both of them were laughing as though they would never stop.

And looking from one to the other, still a bit bewildered

207

but beginning to fear that he saw daylight, was young Sir Thomas, who had slipped to his feet off Pagan and was standing by the chestnut's head.

' Ha, ha, ha,' laughed the boy, doubled up with the sheer animal excess of mirth.

' Ho, ho, ho,' Geoffrey echoed him, knowing that it was all nonsense ; but knowing also that nonsense, just pure, plain nonsense, is the most valid and the oldest reason for mirth in the world.

Now primitive laughter such as that is an infectious thing, yet young Sir Thomas stood looking from one to the other of them, a man undecided. He was betwixt and between. It would have been just as easy for him to fly off into the anger of offended dignity as it was to slide down into the bottomless pit of helpless unreasoning laughter.

He chose the laughter ; or rather, the laughter chose him, so infectious and inescapably did the other two give out their mirth. But it was a near choice, and as soon as breaths were drawn and tears wiped from eyes and talk began to be rational again it was he who spoke first with :

' Nay, but what game is this ? '

' Part of the evening's entertainment, young Sir Thomas ; a little bit of play-acting.'

The young knight nodded. ' Not very convincing really,' he said. ' It's a poor actor who must keep in the shadows, wrapped up, and not speak above a whisper.'

' That was my maidenly modesty.'

' And the letter—that was your doing too ? '

' We were rather proud of that.'

Young Sir Thomas paused and ruminated for a second or two, then he said : ' I recognized your nag, though.'

' You did. You were smart about that.'

' You'll never catch me out over a horse.'

' We couldn't veil the horse, you see.'

' No, just so. And now, what next ? '

' What should be next ? Beer at the Seven Stars, say I.'

' Ay, that, surely, in time. But I think there must be something else first.'

' As for instance ? '

' You two have had your sport and I'll allow it was exceeding funny ; but I'll also claim that it came mighty close to touching one's honour. All sport must be paid for, you know. It must be seen who's the better man.'

Geoffrey looked at him long and steadily.

' Shall we joust with one another then ? ' he asked at length, ' or have sword play ? '

' It might be that we should.'

' I'll wrestle you,' the boy cried, stepping forward, ' willingly.'

A grin of pure delight instantly spread over young Sir Thomas's face.

' Done,' he shouted. He didn't really want anything too serious to come out of the evening's fun, even though he had been scored off in the matter. But he did want some chance of getting his own back and re-establishing himself somehow ; and wrestling was his favourite sport.

' Wrestle we will,' he cried. ' You and I. It was you and I who ran to quieten her palfrey when it took fright at the bear, and we were both of equal service. Let's put it to the test now and see who carries the palm. And the one who does earns the right to go on to the Manor and serenade her this very evening if he so desires.'

' Agreed,' the boy said. ' I'd like nothing better.'

' Ay. Maybe you would like it,' young Sir Thomas took him up a bit grimly, ' but you'll not be riding on to Dalecombe Manor tonight, that I can promise you—unless you know something extra special in the way of holds and falls.'

'Tide what betide,' the boy laughed cheerfully, beginning to strip off his cotte and to kick off his shoes.

Geoffrey, who had kicked off his feminine disguise by now, took charge of all three horses, and young Sir Thomas folded his embroidered cotte very carefully and laid it neatly across Pagan's saddle.

'The best of three bouts?' he said, turning to face the boy, 'and three grasses to decide a bout?'

'Suits me.'

'No Devon or Cornish stuff,' young Sir Thomas warned.

'I'm not uncouth,' the boy answered sharply. 'Somerset style or nothing.'

'And your friend here to play judge—let's hope he does it as well as he played the lady.'

So the two young men stood facing one another in the moonlight, their arms held out at their sides ready for the first play.

Geoffrey waited a few seconds so that both should be equally ready and there should be no favour, and then called : 'Lay holt,' and the first bout was on.

Young Sir Thomas moved so quickly that the boy never knew what grip it was that threw him. But thrown he was ; and in less than no time at all there he was on his back, both shoulder-blades being pressed to the ground while Geoffrey, in his role of judge was calling :

'One, pause, two, pause, three. Grass.'

Young Sir Thomas released his hold and got to his feet, smiling. It was an easy victory, and he liked victories.

But this was only the first grass ; there were yet two more to come, and now the boy was warned. Truth to tell, he rather fancied himself in the wrestling ring, and the ease and speed with which he had just been disposed of had been a shock to him.

'Ready?' Geoffrey called. 'Lay holt.'

This time the boy kept well out of danger and circled warily, keeping a very close watch on his opponent.

There was an old trick, formerly much in use in rings west of Taunton, which he had been taught by a crafty old wrestler, called ' the feint in four '.

It suddenly flashed into his mind to try it, and he put it into action immediately—the half step forward and outwards with the left foot ; the threatening swing of the hip ; the withdrawal and sudden change of feet (which was the essence of the trick) ; and then the *pounce*.

It worked ; he was through his opponent's defences and made his hold.

So far so good. But although he could fall young Sir Thomas, and had felled him, the boy could not grass him. Try as he might he could not force those two shoulder-blades down to the ground—yet.

But he had the advantage and he did not mean to let it slip. Grimly he hung on to his position of attack, bringing into play what additional leverage he could muster ; and every bit as grimly young Sir Thomas, who had been deceived by the feint, but who had not been completely overcome by it, fought to get himself out of the desperate case he was in.

So in the moonlight they struggled till muscles were like to crack under the strain and there was no sound save that of hard-taken breath.

No sound, that is, until a masterful voice startled the wits out of them all by demanding loud and clear :

' Hold then ! What play have we here ? '

So intent were the two contestants on the ground, and so intent also Geoffrey in watching them, that the stealthy arrival of a couple of horses had been unnoticed.

But when Mistress Forester of the Manor House spoke out her query, all three were abruptly and disconcertingly made aware that someone was on the scene. Automatically the boy and young Sir Thomas stopped their striving ; and after a moment's hesitation, both got to their feet somewhat sheepishly.

There was Mistress Forester, that formidable old lady, mounted on her tall black horse ; and behind her, at a respectful four or five paces, Alison on her excitable little palfrey.

'Well,' Mistress Forester continued, realizing now who they were, ' the three young cavaliers of the inn, it seems. Brawling in the moonlight.'

'Hardly brawling, madame,' Geoffrey made bold answer in his easy, assured way. 'There was a—a dispute, and so play was agreed on to settle it.'

'A dispute ? Between gentlemen ? What dispute ? What cause ?'

'The cause of it was fair enough,' young Sir Thomas answered neatly, ' but it's a matter that may now be said to be over,' and so saying, he smiled at the boy and held out his hand to him in the moonlight.

Mistress Forester grunted and looked quickly from one young man to the other. It might be that she guessed something of what was afoot ; it might be that she didn't. She gave no sign, but merely said :

'A good business my lord is kept withindoors with his strained foot. He would have no quarrelling and horse-play by gentlemen in his Manor, I can tell you. After what you told us about it, we had an inclination to ride into Dalecombe and see the entertainment there this evening. Mount your nags, young sirs, and make an escort for us there.'

The three young men needed no further bidding, and they were up on their horses in no time, Geoffrey performing a neat bit of legerdemain to get rid of the girl's dress as he mounted.

It was thus quite a little cavalcade that made its way back into the town, the Lady of the Manor with her daughter riding in front, and, a horse-length behind, their escort of three young men.

The boy rode in the middle of the three. He rode looking straight ahead, not daring to glance to either side. This was because he knew quite well that had he caught the eye of either young Sir Thomas or Geoffrey Chaucer he would have burst out once more into uncontrollable laughter. And he knew by instinct that the other two were feeling just the same ; indeed, there was something ludicrous in the situation, in the mortal terror which the old lady struck into them all ; and in the way in which they were now meekly and silently riding behind her, like chastened schoolboys after their master.

He was thinking about this most of the time ; but there were moments when other thoughts took hold of him—those moments when Alison, riding slim and upright just in front of him, moved her head slightly this way or that and he thought : *it was no delusion. She's just as lovely as I thought she was* ; and his heart turned a little within him for the dream and the desire of life.

When they got to Dalecombe itself it was to find all the townspeople who could afford the price of admission congregated in the inn-yard, and those who had no pennies outside the entrance to it.

The boy had hoped (and so, to tell the truth, had young Sir Thomas) that there might be occasion to do a certain amount of squiring for the beautiful young Mistress Alison ; but all such hopes were rudely cut short by her mother, who had no doubt whatsoever about what she intended to do. Taylor the ostler had appeared as though by magic, and she summoned him to take charge of the horses.

Then she thanked them for their escort ; bade them beware of any further wrestling or rough play ; and with a curt 'good-night' whisked her daughter off into the inside of the Seven Stars, to seek out the host and demand his full attention and hospitality.

The three young men looked in comical dismay at one another ; and at length Geoffrey said : ' So much for the serenading you two were talking about.'

' What an old dragon of a mother ! ' young Sir Thomas exclaimed. ' I'd sooner go into the breaches at Acre than tackle her.'

Geoffrey Chaucer laughed. ' Come on, lads,' he said, ' the world's wide open and there's lots of fun in it. Let's go into the inn-yard and see the sport.'

So they tied their horses to some rings let into the wall, for they saw no chance of getting near the stable for the present, and then pushed their way through the crowd of people thronging the entrance, eventually finding themselves a place in the middle of one side.

At the moment, although there was plenty of noise, nothing was happening. The next turn was to be the performance of the bear, and as nobody in Dalecombe had ever seen a bear before, its appearance was awaited with enormous interest.

The boy, standing between his two companions, looked round the inn-yard with sheer delight. He felt on every side the sense of excitement and expectancy, and he gave a little shiver of pure joy at being part of it. The thought came to him of how right Geoffrey was. ' There's lots of fun in it.'

The moon was now riding high in a sky from which almost every vestige of cloud had disappeared, and the straw-covered centre of the yard was all bathed in silver light. Where the inn itself and the outbuildings cast deep shadow the blackness was lessened by the horn lanterns, which, each with its candle, or in some cases two candles, were swinging from improvised poles and nails and brackets of every sort.

A great deal of beer of one kind or another had been

drunk since the evening began, and most of the noise which was filling the place was due to this primitive but effective cause. Men were laughing and shouting with loosened tongues ; holding up their leather mugs to toast one another across the width of the inn-yard ; or passing them empty from hand to hand over the heads of the crowd, back to the open door of the tap-room for replenishment.

Eli, the Jew from Lincoln, had shut up his stall. Experience had taught him that when the Christians became noisy they were apt to look for something to make sport of ; and not infrequently that something would be the well-stocked stall of a Jew, which could be plundered with comparative impunity. So Eli, the prudent, sad-faced Jew, put up the shutters to his stall and stood by it watching with his sardonic and disillusioned eyes the world take its curious pleasure.

Next to his stall, and towering fantastically high above it like some giant or troll of ancient legend, stood the man on stilts ; or rather, it would be truer to say, swayed the man on stilts, for very foolishly, considering the nature of his employment, he had had as much to drink as anybody else—and as a result he was none too secure on his high perch. He had armed himself with one of the horn lanterns, and as he swayed slightly the motion sent exaggerated shadows dancing and shifting below him all the time.

One end of the yard was, of course, bounded by the inn itself, and here there were two balconies outside the windows of the two principle bedrooms. When one of the Guilds presented a Morality play, or there was any spectacle in the yard, as there was tonight, these balconies were always occupied by favoured guests ; and now, sure enough, the host could be seen ushering into the one on the left Mistress Forester of the Manor House and her daughter Alison.

The boy, looking steadfastly up at her, wondered if she could see him across the yard, and in the end decided regretfully that she couldn't ; after all, he was standing in shadow and it would be difficult to pick out him and his companions from the crowd around. Not that he cared very much one way or the other about his companions in this particular matter, it must be confessed !

The hubbub fell away suddenly as the man in charge of the bear pulled away the sacking which had been put up round the animal and led it at the end of its chain into the centre of the yard.

Normally he would have kept it on the chain, but long familiarity had made him contemptuously forgetful of the fact that a wild animal is always, at heart, a wild animal, and therefore always potentially dangerous. But the bear-keeper too had taken his full share of the evening's conviviality and was laxer than usual. So now he slipped the chain from off the collar of the bear, and prodded it hard in the ribs with his stick to make it realize what was wanted of it. Mechanically the poor beast rose on its hind legs, ready to perform its so-called ' dance ', which was really no more than an ungainly shuffle.

' *The bear, the bear.*' The excited call ran round the now tensely watching crowd and, innocent enough call though it might be, it caused disaster.

The sailor from Dartmouth, who had been sitting in the tap-room on a low stool, legs outstretched, keeping the whole company amused with his spate of tales and reminiscences, and all the time performing manfully with the best ale the Seven Stars could provide, had declared more than once his strong desire to see the bear perform.

Now, therefore, when he heard the half-whisper, half-cry flash round the crowd, he jumped up from his stool in the very middle of a story and rushed clumsily out of the door.

Just outside the doorway of the tap-room he slipped, stumbled, and caught at the nearest thing to steady himself.

217

As luck would have it the nearest thing was not the pole which, for a split second, the tipsy sailor had thought it to be, but instead the left stilt of the man who was standing high above the sailor's head. He, poor man, never stood a chance. You may be the best performer on stilts in the world; but when, without the slightest warning, a sailor weighing sixteen stone clutches at one of your slender props for support, down you come, willy-nilly.

Which was exactly what the man on stilts did. He just had time to let out a yell which was almost equally composed of protest, fear, and rage; and then he came crashing down to earth in no half-hearted manner.

That caused commotion and clatter enough, but the laughter and shouts that greeted it had hardly begun before a very different note rang out in them.

' *The straw, the straw! Fire, fire!* '

The man who had been on stilts lay on the ground groaning; but nobody was paying any attention to him. His horn lantern had come down with him and its two candles, falling out into the dry straw on the inn-yard, had suddenly made the whole situation a very different one.

Flames were already running in the straw and a woman standing with her child right in the front was shrieking:

' *The bear!* '

The shout, and the fear in it, caught everybody's ear, jerked up everybody's head.

The stilt-man in his fall had collided directly with the man in charge of the bear and had sent him flying. This in itself, to say nothing of the general clatter and confusion, had already startled the animal; and when suddenly at its very feet that ancient, most dreaded enemy of the wild—*fire*—broke out, it was no longer startled; it was terrified.

' *The bear, the bear!* '

More than one woman was calling out in fright now and

fighting to get towards the exit of the yard. One or two children, catching that contagious thing, panic, from their elders, echoed their cries of fright ; and to make things worse, people at the back, aware that something exciting was happening but unable to see exactly what it was, began to press forward to find out.

By this time the poor bear itself was overcome with terror. It was much too terrified to want to hurt anybody intentionally ; its one and only aim in life at the moment was to get away from the flames which seemed to be springing up out of the ground all round it.

Moving with surprising speed it lumbered across the open part of the yard and began to swarm up the back part of the inn, making directly, as chance would have it, for the balcony where Mistress Forester and her daughter were sitting.

Like all bears, it was naturally a superbly good climber, and even years of captivity and misery had not made it lose its skill. Moreover, it was just beginning to realize the fact that it *was* free, and possibly fantastic schemes of never being recaptured began to dance in its brain.

There was panic in the yard now. Some men were trying to stamp out the flaming straw, some were shouting for water, some were running to get it, and most of the women were trying in a concerted mass to push their way out of the place and away from the dangerous wild animal.

What the boy realized was that if somebody didn't do something very quickly, the climbing bear would be up in the balcony where the two ladies were sitting.

And when he realized that he acted.

He gave up looking on, and with a startled cry of alarm on his lips began to push and fight his way across the inn-yard.

Young Sir Thomas must have been thinking along the same lines, for simultaneously he started forward too.

But the boy gained the other side of the yard first, beating his rival by a short head. For an instant he stood and looked up. The bear was directly above him, and it had just about reached the upper balcony. If Mistress Forester and her daughter had either of them been the sort of women to scream they would have been screaming then, for they were both terrified ; and with reason.

Without a further second's delay, the boy put hand and foot to work and went up the wooden support after the bear.

The animal was only a few feet above him and he was up with it in no time. He had learned a certain number of things in the world, but never the correct way to tackle an escaping bear.

However, the animal had a broad iron collar round its neck, and there was no time to lose ; so he didn't worry about the niceties of the situation, but merely grabbed hold of the broad iron collar and tugged at it with all his might, swinging on the back of the bear.

The moment was well judged, for within another couple of seconds the bear must have gained the balcony ; but this sudden weight of some ten stone tugging at the back of its neck was too much for it. The animal made a frantic, last-second clawing motion with its fore-legs and then lost its hold and toppled over backwards into the yard below.

Luckily for the boy they fell clear of one another for he had the sense to let go of the animal's collar as they fell.

The moment the bear touched the ground young Sir Thomas, with the greatest presence of mind, whipped up a piece of sacking which was lying near and threw it over the animal. This shut off from its sight the flames, which in any case were now being stamped out ; and at that moment the whole incident was really over. It had flared up out of nothing ; and now, with equally dramatic suddenness, it leaped back into nothing.

A man laughed a bit uncertainly ; people who had been

pushing and nearly fighting to get out stopped and looked sheepish ; and the whole tension was relaxed.

As for the bear it lay immobile under the sacking. Such momentary visions of freedom as the poor thing may have foolishly indulged in were abruptly over ; it was back in its prison now, defeated.

Its keeper, who had picked himself up by now, came running up, stick in hand and eager to get to work with it. But young Sir Thomas, seeing him, did a thing which earned him the boy's good opinion for ever.

He stuck out a hand, grabbed hold of the stick, and brought the man up short.

'The poor beast's scared enough,' he said. 'He wants none of that.'

'But——'

'No buts,' young Sir Thomas told him. 'Put him on the chain, yes—you should never have let him off. But don't knock him about.'

He caught the boy's eyes and they smiled at one another ; and then the boy, lifting his head, saw that Alison Forester was looking down at him from the balcony. Not only looking down, but smiling at him and lifting her small hand in that fascinating little salute of hers.

He raised his own to wave in reply, and in the action moved something that had fallen across his cheek ; he thought perhaps it was a wisp of straw blown up from the floor of the inn-yard. . . .

. . . . .

He brushed his hand across his face to get rid of the quick little stinging pain and Eleanor called out :

'Hard luck. Did it get you in the eye ? '

Tom laughed. 'No, it's all right. It's nothing. Now we can see if Arabs can jump or not.'

They did jump, the whole dangerous band of them, till

tea-time, when Liza came red-faced and irate to call them into the house (' there's crumpets toasted and that's more than you deserve '), and they all trooped out of Street Meadow.

Tom came last of all, leaving the field bathed in the late afternoon sunlight. The field where time stood still. Where Mansuetus of the XXXth had built the Roman road ; where Hubert de Burgh had come with the Domesday Book ; where the Canterbury pilgrims had passed by. And who knows ? Perhaps in some yet later age, another boy might come there, and, suddenly remembering, find himself taking part in the rehearsal of a Band of Arabs for a Pony Club Gymkhana of long ago.